A Note from Lucy Daniels

Dear readers,

I'm so excited that Hodder Children's Books is publishing your favourite titles as Animal Ark Classics. I can't believe it's ten years since Mandy and James had their first adventure. I've written so many stories about them they feel like real friends to me now and it's been such fun thinking up new stories for them both.

I know from your letters how much you enjoy sharing their love of animals. As you can tell, I'm a huge fan of animals myself, and can't imagine a day when I will ever want to stop writing about them.

Happy reading!

Very best wishes,

Lucy

More Animal Ark Classics
from Hodder Children's Books:

Kittens in the Kitchen
Pony in the Porch
Dolphin in the Deep
Bunnies in the Bathroom
Puppies in the Pantry
Hamster in a Hamper
Horse in the House
Badger in the Basement
Cub in the Cupboard
Guinea-pig in the Garage

LUCY DANIELS

ANIMAL ARK
CLASSICS

HORSE in the HOUSE

**Hodder
Children's
Books**

a division of Hodder Headline Limited

Special thanks to Susan Bentley
Thanks also to C. J. Hall, B.Vet.Med., M.R.C.V.S., for reviewing the
veterinary information contained in this book.

Animal Ark is a trademark of Working Partners Ltd
Text copyright © 1998 Working Partners Ltd
Created by Working Partners Ltd, London W6 0QT
Original series created by Ben M. Baglio
Illustrations copyright © 1998 Jenny Gregory

First published in Great Britain in 1998
by Hodder Children's Books
This edition published in 2004

A Catalogue record for this book is available from the British Library

ISBN 0 340 87709 X

Typeset in Baskerville by Avon DataSet Ltd,
Bidford-on-Avon, Warwickshire

Printed and bound in Great Britain by
Clays Ltd, St Ives plc

The paper and board used in this paperback by Hodder Children's
Books are natural recyclable products made from wood grown in
sustainable forests. The manufacturing processes conform to the
environmental regulations of the country of origin.

Hodder Children's Books
a division of Hodder Headline Limited
338 Euston Road
London NW1 3BH

One

'Here you are, Dad,' Mandy Hope said, placing the bag of carrot sticks on the dashboard of the Landrover. 'I cut these up for you.'

'How kind!' Adam Hope said with a grin. He eyed the carrots without much enthusiasm. 'Oh, well. I expect they'll stave off the hunger pangs.'

'Yes. And then you won't be tempted to stop and buy chocolate in Walton, before we get to the horse auctions!' Mandy said promptly.

Her dad was on a diet, but he was terrible at sticking to it. Above his dark beard, his face was red and shiny. Earlier that morning Mandy had heard him huffing and puffing on his exercise bike.

'Hear that, James?' Mr Hope said. 'She's got it all worked out.'

James chuckled. 'She usually has!'

Mandy's best friend sat in the back seat. He had been invited to go to the horse auctions with Mandy and her dad, who was overseeing the horses for sale.

'All set?' Mr Hope steered the Land-rover down the front drive and past the wooden sign which read, 'Animal Ark, Veterinary Surgery'.

'Have a good time!' Mandy's mum, Emily Hope, waved them off. She was standing outside the old stone cottage.

'Bye, Mum! See you later,' Mandy called out.

Emily Hope smiled, her long red hair stirring in the warm breeze.

'Oh! And good luck!' Mandy yelled with a grin.

With a final wave, Mrs Hope went into Animal Ark, where morning surgery was about to start. Mandy's parents were both vets with a joint practice in the village of Welford.

'Why did you wish your mum good luck?' James asked, looking puzzled.

'Because Mrs Ponsonby's bringing Pandora in first thing this morning!' Mandy exclaimed.

'Cripes!' said James. 'She's going to need it then.'

Mrs Ponsonby was a large, imposing woman, who doted on her overweight Pekinese. Mandy imagined her sailing into the surgery, wearing one of her flowery hats, the little dog under one arm.

'You must look at my darling Pandora at once,' Mandy said, in imitation of Mrs Ponsonby's rich, bossy voice. 'My precious poppet's looking extremely off-colour.'

'That Ponsonby woman,' Mr Hope said, shaking his head. 'It's bound to be the usual story. Nothing wrong with Pandora that keeping to a sensible diet wouldn't cure.'

'Hmm. Some people have no will power, have they?' Mandy said. 'Want a carrot stick, Dad?'

Mr Hope coughed and gave his daughter one of his lopsided smiles.

The Land-rover rounded a bend, and the cottage, with its modern vets' extension at the rear, disappeared from view. In the lane that led up to the Fox and Goose crossroads, creamy blossoms dotted the hedgerows.

'Don't you just love spring?' James said, looking out at the fields and the lambs capering about, their black tails flicking back and forth.

'Yep. Almost as much as having school holidays!' Mandy joked. 'Isn't it great? We've got days and days to do anything we like.'

'Like spend them with the animals at Animal Ark,' James said. 'That's what you like best!'

Mandy smiled to herself. She knew it was what James liked best too, even if he *did* sometimes pretend he was more interested in computers.

Mr Hope drove into Welford, then slowed the Land-rover as the road out of the village climbed and narrowed into winding bends.

'There doesn't seem to be anyone at Bennetts' Riding Stables,' Mandy said, as they approached a little stone cottage that stood at the roadside on the outskirts of Welford.

Over the past month, she and James had been helping Wilfred Bennett out at the stables, while his wife, Rose, had been ill in hospital. Sadly, Rose Bennett had died a few weeks ago. Mandy craned her neck. The paddock beyond the cottage and the cluster of stable buildings looked forlorn and deserted. There was a 'For Sale' sign up near the road.

'Look at that,' said James. 'They've put a "Sold" notice over the sign!'

'Yes. Sam Western's bought the Bennetts' land,' Mr Hope informed him. 'He didn't waste any time. Knowing that man, he's already got plans for the place.'

'But what will Wilfred do now?' Mandy was worried about their elderly friend. Surely Sam Western, the wealthy owner of Upper Welford Hall, wouldn't turn Wilfred Bennett out of his home.

'Don't worry, love,' Mr Hope said, munching away

at a carrot stick. 'Wilfred still has his cottage. He'll have a comfortable retirement. I expect we'll see him at the auctions with his horses. They're up for sale today.'

'Oh.' A shadow was cast over Mandy's good mood. 'Do all the Bennetts' horses have to be sold? Even dear old Matty? She was Rose's favourite.'

Mandy was very fond of Matty too. After she and James had learned to ride at Bennetts' Stables, Mandy had usually chosen the gentle silver-grey horse as her mount.

'I bet Wilfred hates having to sell Matty,' James chipped in. 'She was born at the stables, wasn't she?'

'Yes,' Mandy agreed. 'Rose said she delivered Matty herself.'

As she imagined Rose Bennett bending over Matty, a newborn foal with long spindly legs and huge dark eyes, Mandy felt a tug at her heart. It was awful to think that they might never see Matty again after today's horse sale.

Mr Hope glanced across at Mandy. 'Don't look so glum, love. I'm sure all the Bennetts' horses will find good homes, including Matty. And I'll be there to see that everything's in order.'

Mandy had a sudden idea. 'Maybe Wilfred could keep his horses – if he had an extra helping hand or two,' she suggested. 'James and I could carry on helping with the chores around the stables,' she said eagerly. 'We wouldn't mind, would we, James?'

James nodded in agreement.

'I'm afraid that wouldn't make any difference,' Mr Hope said gently.

'What do you mean?' Mandy asked.

'Well,' Mr Hope explained, 'it's not just help that Wilfred needs – it's money. The Bennetts gave away a lot of free riding lessons to people who couldn't afford them, such as groups of disabled children and adults.'

'I remember,' Mandy said. 'That was really nice of them.'

Mr Hope nodded. 'Yes, it was. Everyone in the area admired the Bennetts. But I'm afraid they've been too kind for their own good. They had no head for business and got into rather a lot of debt. The stables hadn't been paying their way for some time, but no one knew about it. It's only come out since Rose died. I was as surprised as anyone to hear about how much money Wilfred owes.'

'Oh.' Mandy felt sorry for Wilfred. First his wife had died, and now this. 'He must have been so worried.'

'But couldn't Wilfred have borrowed some money?' James asked, practical as usual. 'People get bank loans for all sorts of things.'

Mr Hope shook his head. 'Things had gone too far for that. The land had to be sold to pay off Wilfred's debts.'

'So he hasn't anywhere to keep horses now,' Mandy stated, her spirits sinking into her boots. 'Even if he wanted to.'

Matty was quite old now, she thought worriedly. The poor old thing might have difficulty settling into a new home. For one wild moment, Mandy thought of asking her dad if he would buy Matty, but she immediately dismissed the idea. Her parents had strict and sensible rules about having pets and taking in strays.

'Cheer up, love. You have to get used to animals moving on.' Mr Hope's voice was kind, but firm. 'As vets we can't afford to get too attached to them.'

'I know.' Mandy nodded miserably. Her dad was right, but it wasn't always easy to take good advice.

The sun-lit stone cottages and farm buildings along the road to Walton sped by. Wild flowers were nodding on the verges and the gorse was ablaze with bright yellow flowers. Deep in thought, Mandy hardly noticed. The next thing she knew, they had driven into Walton and Mr Hope was parking the Land-rover at the auctions in the space reserved for the visiting vet.

'Golly! There are an awful lot of people here,' James said.

'Yes,' Mandy agreed, looking around at the horse boxes and expensive-looking modern transporters that were packed closely together. Stable boys were ushering horses from their boxes and walking them back and forth to warm up their cramped muscles.

'All right now, Mandy?' Mr Hope said, ruffling his daughter's shortish blonde hair.

She smiled up at him. 'I will be, once I know that all the Bennetts' horses have gone to good homes.'

'That's my girl. Look, there's Wilfred,' Mr Hope said, raising his hand in greeting to Wilfred Bennett as they approached the lorry park.

Mandy saw that the old man's face looked sad and drawn. His straggly white hair was hidden beneath a checked cap. He wore a battered overcoat and woollen muffler and his shoulders were hunched as if he was cold, although there was hardly even a breeze.

Despite the difficult situation, Mr Hope and Wilfred shook hands warmly and exchanged a few words.

'Now then, you two young 'uns.' Wilfred even managed a shaky smile for Mandy and James.

'Hi, Wilfred,' they chorused.

'I didn't get much of a chance to thank you for

helping me out at the stables over these past weeks while Rose was in hospital,' Wilfred said. He spoke slowly, as if the words were an effort, but he was determined to get them out. 'I want you both to know that I really appreciated your help. I know Rose did too. She was glad to know that the horses were in such good hands – especially her Matty.'

'That's all right,' said James. 'We liked helping. Didn't we, Mandy?'

'Of course we did,' Mandy replied. It had been hard work, but worth it, to see the horses and ponies were comfortable.

Wilfred smiled, though his eyes were sad. 'You two had some happy times at Bennetts', didn't you? Especially with our Matty. Though you weren't too keen to ride her at first, eh, James lad? Even though the dear old girl's as gentle as a lamb.'

James flushed, then he grinned. 'Mandy persuaded me to have riding lessons. I'm still not very good, but I enjoyed it.'

Mandy had a lump in her throat and had to take a deep breath before she could speak. She swallowed hard and forced herself to look up at Wilfred. 'I'm so sorry about Rose and I'm sorry that you have to sell your horses,' she said, searching for the right words.

'Thank you, lass. I appreciate your concern. I'm

sorry too,' Wilfred said, the tight line of his mouth softening. 'But there's no help for it. The horses have to be sold and that's an end to it.'

Mr Hope patted the old man's shoulder sympathetically, then said in his usual straightforward way, 'Are you sure you're up to this, Wilfred? I can take care of things for you if you'd like me to. It's really no trouble.'

Mandy realised that her dad meant to be kind, but somehow she knew that Wilfred was going to refuse his offer of help.

Wilfred lifted his cap and smoothed back his hair, then he set the cap more firmly on his head. 'Thanks, lad. I appreciate the offer, but I'm staying with the horses to see them on their way. I owe them that much.'

'Fair enough. I understand,' Mr Hope said. 'Well then, I'd better get on. The auction's about to start. I'm needed for a while, but I'll make sure I see you before I leave.'

'Right you are,' Wilfred said, shortly. The closed-up expression was back on his face. He nodded briefly at Mandy and James, then moved away.

Mandy stared after Wilfred, until his stooped figure had been swallowed up by the crowd. She understood why he wanted to stay and see his horses sold, even if it did almost break his heart. She would have wanted to do the same thing.

'He's a proud old man,' said Adam Hope. 'They don't make them like that any more.'

Mandy and James followed Mr Hope as he led the way towards the pens and the clutch of buyers who were gathering ready. He reached into the pocket of his coat, pulled out a typed list, and passed a cursory glance down the various lots.

'Hmm. It's going to get pretty hectic around here, once the bidding starts,' he said to Mandy and James. 'You two stay put behind the barrier. It's safest there and I'll know where to find you. I'll see you after the sale.'

'OK, Dad,' Mandy said.

She and James found themselves a good viewing point near the sale ring. The holding pens, where the horses were examined and given some last minute grooming by their owners, were some distance away. Mandy couldn't see where Wilfred Bennett was. He was probably over by the holding pens too, she decided, spending every last moment he could with his horses.

'First today, we have Caesar, a three-year-old bay gelding . . .' The auctioneer, a portly, red-faced man in a yellow waistcoat, was up on the stand. He looked out over the buyers. 'Who'll start the bidding?'

'. . . Sold! To you, sir!' The auctioneer announced a few minutes later. His hammer hit the gavel and a buyer held up a piece of card with his name written on it.

Mandy and James watched the stable lads lead the next few horses into the sale ring. Metal shoes rang on the hard ground as hooves clip-clopped around the circumference within the barrier. As each horse was sold, another was brought into the ring.

Each time the auctioneer glanced at his list, Mandy expected to hear Matty's name over the loudspeaker.

'It's exciting, isn't it?' said James. 'I mean . . . even though we feel sorry about Wilfred and everything.'

Mandy nodded agreement. 'There are more horses here than at the Welford Show.'

All kinds of horses could be seen, from mild-natured, sturdy Welsh ponies to sleek hot-blooded thoroughbreds. *But none of them is as lovely as gentle silver-coated Matty*, thought Mandy.

Two hours passed before Mandy glanced up at a wall clock. She was beginning to feel hungry. She resisted the temptation to eat the apple that she had snatched hurriedly on the way out of Animal Ark and stuffed in her pocket. It was a goodbye treat for Matty.

'And now the first of a number of horses from

the highly reputable Bennetts' Riding Stables.'

'Here they come at last,' said James. He didn't look excited now, just subdued and rather sad.

Mandy felt the same. She set her shoulders and peered over the barrier.

'We'll begin with Star – a ten-year-old mare.'

As Star was led into the ring, Mandy saw the ripple of interest run through the buyers. 'Who'll start the bidding?' the auctioneer asked again. Mandy tensed. This was it. It might be the last time she saw any of the Bennetts' horses, including Matty. She found herself longing to see her. The bidding for Star was fierce, voices seemed to come from everywhere. Suddenly the hammer hit the gavel. 'To you, sir!' And Star was sold.

'And now we have Socks. Also from the Bennetts' stable. Who'll start me at . . .'

Socks – with the two white feet – pranced around the ring, looking unconcerned about all the fuss. He too was sold quickly. Then came graceful Bella. The bids came thick and fast, while the auctioneer noted each one, tapping at the air with his pen.

'Any more bids? All done? Sold to you, sir!'

'Cripes!' said James. 'They don't hang about, do they?'

'No,' Mandy replied. 'That's because Wilfred's horses are so good.'

It was true. Muscles moved fluidly beneath the glossy coats, heads were held high, and ears pricked intelligently. Despite her feelings about the sale, Mandy felt proud for Wilfred. His horses were so beautiful. 'A credit to him,' her gran would have said.

Mandy wished each horse luck. 'Goodbye. I hope you'll be happy in your new home,' she whispered.

Next to be announced was Wilfred's sturdy brown pony, Treacle. Treacle trotted around the ring, his tail swishing back and forth. Like the horses before him, he was bursting with good health.

'No Matty yet,' James said, echoing Mandy's thoughts.

'No,' she replied, half-dreading, half-longing to catch a glimpse of the grey mare. How many horses was that so far – four? Four more to go.

James tapped her on the arm. 'See that man over there? He's bought all Wilfred's horses up to now.'

Mandy looked across at the man. She read the large card he held up to the auctioneer as he bought Treacle. 'Newcombe,' she read aloud. It wasn't a local name.

'Who is that, Dad?' she asked, when Mr Hope paused for a moment near the barrier during a break in the bidding.

'Jim Newcombe,' Mr Hope answered. 'He owns a

large riding stables near York. He's well-respected and takes excellent care of his horses.'

'Oh.' Mandy was relieved. At least Wilfred's horses would be well-treated.

As the auction resumed, Mr Hope went back over to the pens.

'And now, the fifth horse on sale today from Bennetts' stables,' said the auctioneer over the loudspeaker. 'What am I bid for Blaze – a handsome fifteen-year-old?'

Mandy tightened her fingers on the barrier. Just three more of Wilfred's horses to be sold: William, Honey and Matty. Who would be next? Honey's name rang out and the sandy-coloured mare lifted her head and whinnied as she was led around the ring. There came the sound of the hammer hitting wood again. That was it.

'Two left now,' Mandy breathed. Suddenly, her throat felt tight with unshed tears. It was almost over. She wondered what Wilfred was thinking.

'That Newcombe man's bought Blaze and Honey as well,' James said. 'He must have pots of money.'

'I hope he's got enough left to buy William and Matty too, then,' Mandy responded, crossing her fingers for luck. *I'll give Matty a final hug, when I give her the apple*, she thought.

The loudspeaker crackled into life again. 'And

now the seventh and last of the horses from Bennetts' Stables. William is a nine-year-old gelding . . .'

Mandy's eyes widened in surprise. That couldn't be right. William wasn't the *last* of Wilfred's horses. There was still Matty to come.

'Hey! What's going on?' said James.

'I don't know,' Mandy replied.

They waited expectantly while William was led around the sale ring. The auctioneer acknowledged the last few bids. 'Any more? All done? Sold to Mr Newcombe. That was the final horse from Bennetts' Stables. And now we have Bruce. A Shetland pony . . .'

Mandy looked at James. 'But what about *Matty*?'

He shook his head, as surprised as her.

Mandy was too stunned to react at first. Then the worry began creeping in. Where could Matty be? Suddenly, she knew what she must do: 'I've got to find Wilfred,' she said.

'But your dad told us to stay right here,' James reminded her.

Mandy hesitated. Her dad's instructions had been clear and she didn't want to get into his bad books, but she just had to find out what had happened to Matty.

'Look, Wilfred's only just over there,' she said,

catching sight of the stooped figure. 'I won't be long. I'll be back before Dad comes over here to us.'

Some of the buyers moved back to let her pass, but others glared down at her disapprovingly. Mandy bent and made herself as small as she could and squeezed her way through the crush of people.

It was a few minutes before she managed to get through the crowd. 'Wilfred! Mr Bennett!' she called, in an urgent whisper.

She had to call twice more before Wilfred turned round. He looked dazed, as if he couldn't believe this was really happening.

'Oh, hello, Mandy. You shouldn't be over here, lass. It's a bit hectic around this area.'

'Yes, I know,' she said. 'I'm going back in a minute. But I wanted to ask you . . . Where's Matty? James and I have been watching out for her.'

'Er . . . Matty?' Wilfred's gaze slid sideways, then he took off his cap and began examining it intently.

'Yes. Has she been sold yet?' Surely he couldn't have forgotten about Matty!

'Oh, don't worry about Matty, pet,' Wilfred said, speaking rapidly in a low voice. 'She's going to be fine.'

But Mandy was worried. She couldn't explain it, even to herself, but every bit of her was alert. Something was going on, she just knew it.

'Didn't you bring Matty here with the other horses?' she persisted, having to raise her voice to be heard.

'Hush,' Wilfred said, so low that she had to strain to hear him. Suddenly he looked up, meeting her gaze as if he wanted to impress his words upon her. His faded blue eyes were still as bleak as they had been earlier, but now they shone with determination. 'I told you, pet,' he said, tapping the side of his nose with his index finger. 'I've got other plans for Matty. You mustn't worry. Leave it be.'

With that, Wilfred put his cap back on then turned away and began making a path for himself through the people who were leading the horses towards the exit.

Puzzled by the secretive sign he had made, Mandy was about to hurry after Wilfred and ask him some more questions. But then, a deep voice beside her said, 'Mandy!'

'Oh!' She almost jumped out of her skin. 'Dad!'

'Who were you expecting?' Mr Hope clapped a hand on his daughter's shoulder. 'I thought I asked you and James to stay together! A busy auction is not a place to go wandering around.'

'Yes, I know, Dad . . .' Mandy began. 'I'm sorry, but I just had to . . .'

Mr Hope sighed. 'Don't tell me. I know that look

on your face. I might have known. Animals always come first with you. You're worried about Wilfred's horses, aren't you?'

Yes – she was worried, but only about one particular horse now – Matty. Mandy wanted to know what Wilfred had meant when he said he had 'special plans' for the silver-grey mare. She sighed, and nodded.

'Come along, love,' Mr Hope said. 'Let's get back to James. We've almost finished here anyway. Wilfred's horses all have a good home. We must be content with that.'

Mandy bit her lip and fell into step with her father. 'But that's just it, Dad. Not all of Wilfred's horses have been sold today – what about Matty?'

Mr Hope stroked his dark beard thoughtfully. 'Now that you come to mention it, I don't recall checking her over with the other horses.'

'Why don't you look at your list?' Mandy suggested. 'If Matty was in the auction her name will be on it.'

'Good idea.' Mr Hope reached into his coat pocket and took out a crumpled piece of paper. He smoothed it out and scanned down the columns of owners' and horses' names. After a few moments he frowned. 'You're right. Matty's name's not listed. How odd.'

'I knew it!' Mandy said, though Matty's name being missing from her dad's list explained nothing. Matty had to be somewhere. But where?

Two

'Are you going to go up to Wilfred's cottage today?' Mandy asked her dad, a couple of days after the horse sale. She was eager for news of the old man, and, more particularly, for an explanation about Matty.

Adam Hope shook his head as he poured himself a cup of tea. 'I've been meaning to go and see him, but we've had a run of emergencies. I was up at Greystones Farm all yesterday morning. Nelson, the Gills' boar, slipped in the mud and injured his leg.'

The boar was a British Saddleback: very handsome with his piebald black and white colouring and big floppy ears. He was also enormous, weighing about two hundred kilos.

'Poor Nelson,' Mandy said. 'Was the leg broken?'

'No,' her dad replied. 'It was a green-stick fracture: the bone was partly broken and partly bent. I put a cast on and gave a sedative.' He flashed her a grin. 'Nelson didn't seem too grateful!'

Emily Hope was buttering her toast. 'There was another emergency at Baildon Farm. One of Jack Mabson's Jerseys had a nasty case of bloat.'

'Which one?' Mandy asked, worriedly. 'Not Goldie, was it?'

Mrs Hope smiled. 'No. The little calf you named is fine. It was Patsy. I gave her a drench of peanut oil in warm water and she was much better by the time I left. I'm going up to Baildon Farm today to check that she's OK.'

'Oh,' Mandy was relieved. It was certainly busy at Animal Ark. With her mum out on call and her dad in the surgery, it didn't look as if anyone would have time to call in on Wilfred.

Mandy got up from the table and took her breakfast plate over to the sink. Her parents might not have time to visit Wilfred, but she and James had. 'I'll just do my chores and look in on Bonny before I meet James,' she said, making a dash for the door.

Bonny was a Toy Poodle who had been admitted with a badly cut foot. She was Mandy's favourite patient at the moment. Mrs Hope had suspected cut tendons, but she had operated and found the tendons undamaged. She had managed to repair the torn pads. Now Bonny was doing fine.

In the residential unit, Mandy mopped floors, cleaned out cages and changed water dishes. The work wasn't very exciting, but it had to be done. She thought about Wilfred as she finished her chores. Maybe he'd feel more like talking about Matty today.

After washing her hands, she opened Bonny's cage. 'Hello, girl,' she said, taking the little dog out. 'How are you feeling today?'

As Mandy stroked the tightly curled fur, Bonny gave a friendly whine and licked her on the chin. 'You'll be going home soon,' Mandy said. Bonny gave a soft woof, as if she understood everything Mandy said. *She probably does*, thought Mandy, with a grin; poodles were very intelligent dogs.

Back in the Animal Ark reception area, Mandy glanced at the wall clock. It was almost time for morning surgery. *Time to go and meet James*, she thought, and went to find her mum and dad to tell them she was leaving.

Adam Hope's voice floated out of the open examination room door. 'I'm not surprised that Sam Western snapped up the old Bennett place,' he was saying to his wife. 'You have to give it to that man, he knows a good thing when he sees it.'

As Mandy walked into the room, Emily Hope nodded. 'He's probably the only farmer around here wealthy enough to raise the money at short notice.' She was taking packs of sterile dressings from a cupboard.

Mandy went over and held open the cupboard door to help her mum. 'Thanks, love,' Mrs Hope said. 'Could you put a few of these over there?'

'Do you think Mr Western will farm Wilfred's old land?' Mandy asked.

'I expect he might,' her dad said. 'He's the sort who always has an eye towards expansion. You can bet that he sees his new purchase strictly as a business proposition.'

Everyone in Welford knew that Sam Western prided himself on having the most modern machinery in his milking sheds. He had annoyed quite a few people in the past with his pompous manner.

'We'll just have to wait and see, I suppose,' Mrs Hope said, going to the sink to wash her hands with anti-bacterial fluid. 'No sense in us worrying about it.'

Mr Hope half-turned away and sneaked a snack-sized chocolate bar from his coat pocket. Mandy eyed the chocolate bar. So much for his latest diet.

'Dad! That's millions of calories. How could you? And straight after breakfast, too.'

'It's only a tiny one, hardly more than a biscuit,' Mr Hope said, innocently raising his eyebrows until they almost disappeared into his dark hair. 'Besides a bit of junk food now and then gives the old immune system a boost.'

'Oh, right.' Mandy pulled a face, unconvinced. She glanced at her mum and inclined her eyes heavenwards.

Mrs Hope returned the gesture. 'He'll be out jogging up towards the Beacon at the weekend, trying to run the calories off! I hope you're ready to go with him on yet another training session.'

'That's it, you two! Gang up on me.' Adam Hope affected a hurt expression, but his eyes gleamed with good humour. He popped the last of the chocolate into his mouth and chewed defiantly. 'Lovely.'

Just then Jean Knox, Animal Ark's receptionist, popped her greying head around the door. 'Ready for this morning's first patient?' she enquired cheerily.

'I'd better go.' Mandy made a lunge for the door. 'I've got to meet James. Bye, Mum. Bye, Dad. See you later.'

Flying out of Animal Ark, she took her bike from the shed and pedalled briskly down the narrow lane.

James was waiting for her by the bus stop outside the Fox and Goose pub.

'Oh, you've brought Blackie with you!' Mandy laid her bike on the grass verge and knelt down to stroke the Labrador's floppy ears.

Blackie wriggled his body and wagged his thick tail. He pushed his cold wet nose into Mandy's hand, inviting her to fuss him.

'Ow!' James complained as the dog's tail thwacked against his jeans. 'That stings.'

Mandy chuckled. 'Well, you ought to know to get out of the way by now!' Blackie's manners had never been very good and they didn't seem to be improving with age.

'Did your dad call in and ask Wilfred about Matty?' asked James.

Mandy shook her head. 'He's been too busy to go and see him. I thought we could go.'

'Fine by me,' James said, getting on his bike.

They pedalled along the hilly road towards the outskirts of Welford, easing down into bottom gear to tackle the steep inclines. Soon they rounded a bend in the road and saw Wilfred's cottage ahead of them.

'Wow!' James leaned forward on his handlebars and blew a silent whistle. 'Just look at that!'

'Oh!' Mandy came to a halt in a shower of pebbles,

almost falling off her bike with amazement.

A high wooden fence had been erected between the cottage and what was now Sam Western's land, cutting off Wilfred's view of his old stables. It looked very imposing.

'Huh! Someone's been busy!' Mandy said disapprovingly.

'Yeah. And we don't need three guesses who!' muttered James.

From beyond the new fence came the sounds of hammering and sawing.

'What d'you think's happening over there?' asked James.

Mandy shrugged. 'I don't know. Maybe Wilfred does though. We could ask him.'

'Come on,' said James.

They leaned their bikes against the new fence, then knocked on the cottage door. There was no answer. Mandy picked up the horse-shaped knocker and gave three decisive raps. Still nothing. She bent forward and put her ear to the door.

'I can't hear anything.'

'I'm not surprised with that row coming through the fence,' said James. 'Perhaps Wilfred's out shopping.'

'Let's check round the back,' Mandy said. 'Maybe he's left the back door open.'

But the back door was firmly closed and the
yard, a tiny square of concrete hardly big enough
to hold the dustbin, was also empty. Mandy noticed
that the curtains were drawn in the back sitting
room.

'That's funny,' she said.

James frowned. 'What is?'

Mandy pointed to the window. 'Look. Why would
Wilfred close the curtains in the daytime?'

James agreed that it seemed odd. Mandy knocked
on the back door with her knuckles, but there was
still no answer. After a moment, she and James
walked back round to the front of the cottage.

Mandy lifted the door knocker again. 'Let's give
it one last try.'

From the corner of her eye, she thought she saw
a movement at a downstairs window. 'He's in there,
I'm sure of it!'

'Mr Bennett! Wilfred!' she and James chorused.
'It's us, Mandy Hope and James Hunter.'

There was a long pause, then they heard a bolt
being drawn inside the front door. The door opened
a crack and Wilfred Bennett peered out worriedly
from the dark interior. When he saw that they were
alone, his wrinkled old face relaxed.

'Now then, you two young 'uns,' he said, sounding
relieved.

'Hi, Wilfred. We've come to see how you are,'
Mandy said. 'We thought you weren't in.'

'I'm not in to most people,' Wilfred said quietly.
'I don't want bothering, see. I'm best left alone.'

James coloured. 'Sorry. We . . . um . . . just wanted
to ask you about Matty,' he said awkwardly.

Wilfred scratched his head, so that his straggly
white hair stuck up in fluffy tufts. He looked
flustered. 'Right – well, thanks for calling. I'm fine,
really.'

'And Matty?' Mandy coaxed, when it looked as if
Wilfred wasn't going to mention her. 'You said you
had plans for her.'

A panicky expression flickered across Wilfred's
face. 'Did I?'

'Yes,' Mandy said. 'You did.' She was worried.
There was something different about Wilfred. He
seemed jumpy and on edge.

'Dear me now. I'm getting so forgetful.' Wilfred
fiddled with the buttons on his cardigan. 'Well,
anyway,' he said vaguely. 'Like I already told you,
lass. Matty's fine.'

There was an awkward silence, broken by a soft
'woof' from Blackie, who was behaving himself for
once. He sat next to James, his tail thumping in a
friendly fashion, a doggy grin stretching from ear
to ear.

A smile flickered across Wilfred's tired face. For a moment, Mandy thought, he looked like his old self.

'Now then, m'lad.' Wilfred patted the Labrador's broad dark head, smiling at James. 'He's a grand young dog.'

'Wilfred,' Mandy began, encouraged to have one more try. 'About Matty . . .'

Wilfred's face closed down like a shutter. 'Well – I've got to go inside now,' he said quickly. 'I've . . . er . . . got something cooking on the stove. Say hello to your mum and dad for me, Mandy.'

Before Mandy and James could say another word, Wilfred had closed the door, quick as a flash.

'Oh.' Mandy heard the sound of bolts being shot and locks turned. How odd. She had been to the cottage loads of times and the doors had never even been locked, let alone bolted.

James also looked puzzled. 'Did you smell anything cooking?'

'No, I didn't,' Mandy said, still worried. 'Wilfred was acting strangely, wasn't he?'

James nodded, then he shrugged. 'Perhaps it upsets him to talk about Matty,' he suggested reasonably.

That could be it, Mandy thought. Poor Wilfred. But at the back of her mind there was still doubt. Something was wrong.

'Come on,' James said.

'OK,' Mandy replied. 'No point in hanging about round here.'

Blackie followed obediently as they retraced their steps and fetched their bikes. Mandy glanced over her shoulder and thought she saw the curtain at the kitchen window twitch.

'Wilfred's watching, making sure that we leave,' she said to James.

'But why would he do that?'

'I wish I knew,' Mandy said, wheeling her bike on to the road and scooting along with one foot on the pedal.

They moved a few yards along the road, to where they could see into the field. Over the hedge they had a clear view of Wilfred's old paddock and stable buildings.

'Sam Western hasn't knocked them down,' said James. 'I thought he would.'

'He might do yet,' Mandy said, noticing the car and builder's van parked outside the stable block.

Suddenly Blackie barked and leapt forward. He'd seen a rabbit. James made a grab for his collar, but it was too late. The Labrador shot through the nearby open gate and bounded across the field towards the stable block.

'Oh, no!' Mandy gasped. Trust Blackie. He only had to see the white bobtail of a rabbit and he was off.

James pedalled after Blackie like fury, his body bent over the handlebars. 'Quick! We have to catch him.'

Not much chance of that, thought Mandy. The young Labrador was stocky like all his breed, but he could run like a greyhound when he put his mind to it.

'Hang on a sec!' she called, fumbling with her bike in her haste. But James was already halfway to the old paddock; there was nothing to do but follow him.

Outside the stable, there was a muscular workman in overalls, whom neither of them recognised as a local. He watched Mandy and James approach, an amused look on his pleasant face. He pointed towards Blackie, who was now little more than a speck in the distance, and called out jauntily, 'He went that-a way!'

Next to the workman was a second man, who was leaning against a car. Mandy recognised the stern, sharp features at once. It was Dennis Saville, Sam Western's farm manager.

'Uh-oh,' she murmured.

James slowed down. He turned to wait for Mandy

to catch up. 'Do you see who that is?'

Mandy nodded.

Mandy and James had clashed with Dennis Saville before. They knew him to be a humourless, matter-of-fact type, who was only concerned with following his boss's orders.

'I suppose you realise you're trespassing,' Dennis Saville said frowning, as he walked towards Mandy and James.

James reddened. 'We didn't mean to,' he said. 'We're just trying to catch my dog.'

'Obviously,' said Dennis Saville coldly. 'I suggest you call it to heel.'

There's a fat chance of Blackie taking any notice, Mandy thought. She felt embarrassed for James, who could only wait helplessly until Blackie got bored and trotted back by himself.

Luckily, at that moment, Blackie did just that. Having lost the scent of the rabbit, he came panting and lolloping down the field towards them, curious to know what was going on. He went straight up to Dennis Saville, his tail wagging and his face split in one of his silly doggy grins.

Mandy groaned, sensing trouble.

Anybody else would have patted the friendly dog, but not Dennis Saville. 'You'd better put that dog on a lead,' he said shortly, 'if you can't control it.'

Mandy knew that James must be dying to say that Blackie was not an 'it'.

Red to his ears, James got off his bike, collared Blackie and clipped on the lead, saying, 'His name's Blackie.' Lowering his voice so that only Mandy could hear, he added, 'You should know that! You've met him before.'

'I don't care what it's called,' Dennis Saville replied. Then, turning to Mandy, he said, 'What are you doing out here, anyway? You're the vets' daughter, aren't you?'

While Mandy nodded, James glared at the man in silence.

'We came to visit Wilfred,' Mandy explained. 'He's our friend.'

Dennis Saville nodded. 'I remember the old man telling my boss that you kids helped him out with the horses when his wife was ill in hospital. Well, this place won't be used as stables any more.'

'What's it going to be used for then?' James asked, curiosity triumphing over his anger.

At first Mandy thought Dennis Saville wasn't going to reply. It would be just like him to tell James to mind his own business. The big man in overalls, who had been watching in silence until now, winked at Mandy and James, then spoke to Dennis Saville.

'I'm putting the sign up later,' he said mildly.

'Everybody will soon know about your boss letting the field to campers.'

'A campsite?' Mandy whispered, looking at James.

Dennis Saville glanced sharply at the burly workman. He looked as if he might be about to tell the man not to interfere, then he shrugged.

'Show them what you've been doing, if you like,' he said. 'But don't waste too much time. I've got business to attend to. I'll be back later.'

Silently, James mouthed, 'Wow!'

Mandy was speechless. Wonders would never cease; Dennis was being almost human for once.

Dennis Saville strode over to his car and got in. 'Just a quick look inside, mind,' he said from the open window. 'And tie that dog up outside.'

'OK,' said James, too surprised even to feel cross any more.

As Dennis Saville's car disappeared through the open gate, the workman reached down to pat Blackie. 'Hello, boy. You're a friendly one, aren't you?' He gave a small toss of his head in the direction of the gate. 'Not much of a dog lover that Dennis Saville, is he?'

'Huh! He likes Sam Western's nasty bulldogs all right!' said James. 'Horrible things.'

'It's not the bulldogs' fault.' Mandy couldn't help speaking up. She loved all animals, and knew that if dogs were wary and hostile, then usually the owners were at fault. 'Sam Western's trained them to be that way.'

'That's true,' James admitted.

Once inside the stable block Mandy and James stared in amazement. The place smelled of new paint and sawdust. The workman had been busy painting the ceiling and walls white. Six of the eight stalls had been fitted with doors and against one wall there were two tiled washbasins with mirrors above them.

'What do you think?' the workman said. 'Makes a good shower and toilet block, doesn't it?'

'Yes,' Mandy agreed politely. 'Very smart.'

She looked wistfully at the two stalls which had been left empty. Not long ago she and James had been mucking them out, spreading fresh new bedding, and filling hay nets for Wilfred's horses. Instead of fresh paint and the noise of hammering there had been the sounds of horses shifting contentedly in their stalls and the smell of saddle soap and hoof oil.

And, best of all, there had been the feel of Matty's soft mouth as she had gently taken the crunchy red apple from her hand.

WESTERN'S CAMPSITE

Three

The following morning Mandy was helping her dad treat a baby hedgehog with an infected foot. Betty Hilder, who ran the local animal sanctuary, had brought the little animal into Animal Ark. It was part of a litter that had been found in a barn, after the mother was killed on the road.

'Yes,' Betty was saying, 'I saw definite signs of badgers in the woods at the back of Wilfred Bennett's old place. I was planning to release two rescued hedgehogs up there, Susie and Tess. But I've changed my mind now.'

'Lucky for Susie and Tess!' Mr Hope said. 'Badgers are one of the few animals capable of tackling a hedgehog.'

'Exactly,' Betty said. 'I'm pleased to see badgers

moving back into the woods, but I'm going to have to find somewhere else to release my hedgehogs.'

'Wouldn't it be wonderful if a whole colony of badgers moved in?' Mandy said, her eyes shining. She held the hedgehog gently but firmly as Mr Hope tipped antibiotic powder on to the cleaned foot.

'A whole cete of them would be even better,' her dad replied.

'Dad! That's the same thing as a colony!'

Mr Hope gave her one of his lopsided smiles. 'Just testing,' he said.

Betty Hilder chuckled. 'You can't trick Mandy! How's little Midge doing? Will she need to stay here?'

'What a lovely name! It really suits her,' Mandy said. Midge made snuffling noises and her pointed nose wrinkled as she sniffed at the air. Her spines were still faintly pink and quite soft. 'She's so tiny.'

'Compared to Susie and Tess, she is,' Betty agreed. 'Those two are a couple of bruisers! It's hard to believe they were this small when they came to me.'

Mr Hope smiled. 'I think you can take Midge back to the sanctuary. She's thriving on being hand-fed. If you're at all worried about that foot, give me a call.'

'Thanks. I will.' Betty gathered Midge up and put her back into a straw-lined box. Almost before Betty

Hilder was out of the door, Mandy had shrugged off her white lab coat. Washing his hands at the sink beside her, Mr Hope smiled. 'Thanks for your help, love. I don't need three guesses to know where you're off to now.' His dark eyes twinkled. 'Nice day for a walk in the woods!'

Mandy flashed her dad a grin as she left the treatment room. If a badger family *had* moved back into the deserted setts, she definitely wanted to know about it.

'Wow!' said James, when Mandy told him. 'Let's go up there right now.'

Mandy grinned. 'I thought you'd say that. What about Blackie?'

'Not a good idea!' said James. 'Dogs and badgers don't mix very well!'

He looked thoughtful. Mandy knew that he hated leaving Blackie behind.

James's face brightened. 'I've just remembered. Mum's got a friend coming round who always brings Blackie's favourite dog biscuits. I don't think he'll mind staying at home – just this once!'

The sun shone brightly as they pedalled through Welford village. At the edge of the woods, they took one of the bridleways that snaked through the trees. After a spell of wet weather the woods were ablaze with many shades of green.

'This is near the place,' Mandy said after a while. 'We have to leave the bikes here.'

They made their way up the hillside on foot. Dappled light flickered through the trees and the rich smell of leaf mould rose from beneath their feet.

'This seems like a good look-out spot,' whispered James, crouching down behind a tangle of branches. 'Let's use these bushes for cover.'

'Yes,' Mandy agreed, dropping down beside him. She felt like a commando as she squirmed forward, using her elbows and knees.

She peered through the brambles. Directly in front of her, the ground dipped sharply away to a basin-shaped hollow. Beneath twisted tree roots and the yellowing stalks of bluebells and primroses, the slopes were honeycombed with entrances to disused setts.

'I don't expect we'll see any badgers,' whispered James. 'Even though they sometimes come out in the daytime.'

'No,' Mandy said, craning her neck. 'I bet they're safe underground, all curled up in their grassy nests.' It sounded cosy, but she knew badgers faced many dangers from men and dogs.

James squinted against the sun, which was

reflecting off his glasses. He put up a hand to shade his face. 'Did Betty say she definitely saw signs of digging? I can't see a thing.'

'I can!' Mandy whispered excitedly, tugging at his arm. 'Move over here a bit. See?' She pointed to a pile of sandy earth outside a sett halfway up the slope. 'It's a spoil heap! Betty's right. New badgers have moved in.'

'Wow!' said James, settling his glasses more firmly on his nose. 'Isn't it great? I wonder if it's a sow. There might be cubs too.'

Mandy felt excited. 'I hope so. Clever things. They've got ready-made homes in those deserted burrows, and lots of food.'

James nodded. 'That leaf mould looks centimetres deep. I bet it's just teeming with juicy worms and beetles and stuff.'

'Lovely!' Mandy said with a grin. 'Sounds like badger heaven!' Suddenly she was serious. 'We'll have to be really careful who we tell about this. Dad and Betty know already, of course, but they won't tell anyone else.'

'Right,' agreed James, his brows drawn together in a fierce frown. 'It'll be our secret. No one's going to hurt these badgers. Not if we have any say about it!'

Mandy felt a shiver run down her back. They had

once encountered badger baiters, in the shape of Mr Bonser, who owned Old Dyke Farm.

'I can't understand why anyone thinks it's fun to hurt an animal,' she said angrily. 'It's so cruel. I hate all kinds of hunting.'

'Me too,' said James. 'It's a good thing that lots of people agree with us. Most of them really care about animals.'

'That's true,' Mandy said, cheering up as they crept quietly back to the track, where they had left their bikes. She cared a great deal. That's why she wanted to be a vet like her mum and dad when she was older.

They pedalled slowly back along the bridleway, enjoying the warmth of the sun on their backs. Mandy found her thoughts dwelling on Matty. She really missed the elderly little mare. She wondered who owned her now. They were so near Wilfred's cottage that she couldn't resist grasping the chance to call in on him.

'Shall we cycle back past the Bennetts' old field?' she suggested casually. 'We might catch a glimpse of Wilfred. Sometimes he sits in the doorway of his cottage, enjoying the sun.'

She saw that James wasn't fooled one bit. 'Don't tell me. You're after another chance to ask him about Matty.'

'Yep. That's the idea.' Mandy glanced sideways at her friend. James was wearing his serious look. 'What's wrong? Do you think I'm making too much fuss about Matty?'

'No,' James said stoutly, colouring under her direct gaze. 'OK then; maybe a bit,' he admitted. 'I told my dad about the auction and Matty not being there and he said Wilfred must have sold Matty privately.'

'I expect he did,' Mandy agreed, thinking that James's logical explanation still didn't explain why Wilfred was acting so mysteriously. 'I want to know who bought Matty. That's all. If her new owner's not too far away we might be able to go and visit her.'

James grinned. 'Well – you do still owe her a red apple!'

Mandy couldn't help smiling. That was true.

'It's not just Matty. It's Wilfred,' she said after a moment. 'He seems so . . . different somehow. Not just sad and quiet like he has been, but anxious about something.'

She couldn't explain it, even to herself. Wilfred had been so flustered and worried-looking when they visited him a couple of days ago. It just wasn't like him.

James scooted forward and pedalled out from

under the trees. 'Come on then. I don't mind going that way. I want to see what's going on up at the new campsite anyway.'

Mandy knew that James was concerned about Wilfred too, although he hid it better than she did. They free-wheeled down the track to the road, then coasted down the dips. As they rounded the bend on the outskirts of the village they saw the new wooden fence. Wilfred's cottage, only a few metres away from the high fence, looked somehow isolated and cut-off.

'Isn't it a shame?' Mandy murmured. 'All Wilfred has in the world now is his cottage. Instead of green fields and horses he has a boring view of the road.'

'Huh! Look at that,' said James, pointing to the newly erected sign, which read 'Western's Campsite' in bold letters. 'Anybody would think the place was a posh holiday camp instead of an almost bare field.'

It was typical of the pompous landowner Mandy thought. 'Look. The gate's open and there are people in the field.'

Stakes had been hammered into the ground to mark out tent pitches. Mandy and James leaned forward on their handlebars and watched the campers putting up their tents.

'Look at that one. It's like a house,' said James.

In one corner, a trailer tent was slowly being

transformed into a multi-roomed canvas bungalow, complete with floor-length picture windows, canopy and porch. Two adults and two children were unloading a great deal of equipment from a car. There were airbeds, sleeping bags, hang-up wardrobes, and even a cooker. You name it, these campers had got it.

Mandy expected them to unpack a full-size bath at any moment. 'Look. That tent's just the opposite!' she said.

Just inside the gate, a tall, thin woman, wearing a bright red beret, baggy army shorts and walking boots, was erecting a low green tent. Her movements were quick and efficient as she slung a fly-sheet over her tent and began pegging it down. An enormous bulging backpack lay on the grass, and running around it excitedly was a brown and white Jack Russell terrier.

'Sparky, do calm down,' the woman said mildly. The little dog promptly sat. He watched, ears pricked intelligently, as his owner finished pitching the tent. 'That's better. You know I insist on good manners.'

'What an obedient dog,' said James with a trace of longing in his voice.

Mandy knew he was wishing Blackie took the slightest notice of anything he was told. 'Never mind,' she said. 'Blackie understands a few words.'

'Yeah, two of them! "Walk" and "Food"!' James said.

The woman looked up and saw Mandy and James watching. 'Hello, there!' she called cheerily. 'Do you live in the village?'

Mandy nodded. 'I'm Mandy Hope; my mum and dad are vets in Welford. This is James Hunter, my best friend.'

As Mandy and James wandered over, the woman gave a broad grin. 'How do you do,' she said, shaking hands with each of them. 'I'm Flora Pearson and this is Sparky.'

The formal introduction and old-fashioned handshake amused Mandy and she grinned back.

'Pleased to meet you, Sparky,' she said, bending down to stroke the little dog. The Jack Russell's long, undocked tail twirled madly as he rolled on his back, his tongue lolling in a wide grin.

'Really, Sparky! Have you no shame?' Flora said, her eyes sparkling with good humour. 'He absolutely thrives on attention.'

Mandy chuckled. 'What a friendly little dog!'

'Oh, Sparky loves everyone and everything. Except for horses. He's a holy terror with them. I have to call him to heel, otherwise he's off after them like a shot, barking and setting up a fine old racket!'

'He'll be fine here,' Mandy said. 'There were riding stables here once, but not any more. And it's mainly sheep up on the moors.'

'Ah. Sparky has nothing against woolly jumpers!' Flora joked.

Mandy and James laughed with her. 'Do you need any help with your tent?' asked James politely.

'How kind of you to ask,' Flora said. 'But I've just about finished. I was going to make some tea. Would you like to join me? We do so enjoy having visitors, don't we, Sparky?'

Sparky cocked his head and rolled his lips back. He sat up very straight, with his teeth all on show, his eyes wide in a glassy stare.

'Cripes!' James said, not sure what to make of the little dog. 'What's wrong with him?'

'Oh, that's just Sparky's way of smiling,' Flora explained. 'Some people are a bit alarmed when he first does that.'

Mandy wasn't surprised. She laughed. 'Did you teach him that?'

Flora shook her head. 'Oh, no. Sparky did it all by himself. He's very intelligent.'

Mandy and James sprawled on the grass outside Flora's tent, while she boiled water, then spooned tea into a huge enamel pot. Mandy looked across at James. No wonder the backpack was bulging if Flora carried a tea pot and a tin of leaf tea about with her.

'What's she got against tea bags?' James whispered.

Mandy hid a smile. Flora Pearson was a bit strange, but in a nice way. After a moment, Flora delved into the backpack and brought out another square tin and four brightly patterned tin mugs. She poured tea into all the mugs.

James frowned. 'Four?' he mouthed silently at Mandy.

'There you are, Sparky. That's yours,' Flora said. 'Plenty of milk in that one.' She smiled at Mandy and James. 'He always has the yellow mug.'

Mandy and James burst out laughing as the little dog placed one paw either side of the mug, dipped his head and delicately lapped his tea.

'Flapjack anyone?' Flora said, opening the square tin. 'I make them myself. Sparky won't eat shop-bought cakes.'

Of course he won't, Mandy thought. As they drank their tea and munched flapjacks, Flora explained that she was on a walking holiday.

'Sparky and I are just staying here for the night,' she said. 'Tomorrow we're off to explore the fells up past the Beacon.'

'It's lovely up there,' Mandy said. She knew the Celtic cross landmark well. Her dad often went

jogging up that way. 'Brilliant views across the valleys.'

Flora seemed pleased to have found someone with knowledge of the area. She spread a battered Ordnance Survey map on the grass. Smoothing out the creases, she traced the long slope up to the landmark with a thin finger. 'We'll start here, bright and early.'

'Oh, look. There's Upper Welford Hall. Sam Western owns it. He's a local farmer,' Mandy said. 'He owns this campsite too.'

'Really? Do you know everyone around here?' Flora said.

'She should do,' James put in. 'Her mum and dad visit all the farms, even the isolated ones up there.'

Flora gave a delighted laugh. 'Do you hear that, Sparky? We've just invited local celebrities to tea!'

Mandy and James looked at each other. They'd never been called celebrities before. 'We're not famous,' Mandy giggled, liking Flora more by the minute. 'But my friend's mum is. She plays the vicar's wife in *Parson's Close*.' It was her gran's favourite soap on TV.

'Just fancy,' Flora said. 'Sparky loves watching TV.'

Mandy and James exchanged a glance. Of course he did!

After they finished their tea, they offered to fill Flora's water container. 'So kind,' Flora said, handing them what looked like a sturdy, rolled-up plastic bag fixed to a coat hanger. Flora's water storage arrangements were as eccentric as the woman herself!

Sparky scampered up the field with them to the tap outside the old stable block. He sat, head on one side, watching them as water gushed into the container, making it swell into a pot-bellied shape. Then he walked beside them, back down the field, trotting obediently at heel.

'Good boy,' said James, looking down at the little dog. He smiled across at Mandy. 'I think he's guarding Flora's home-made water carrier. As if anyone would want to steal it!'

'Thanks,' Flora said on their return. She hung the container from a low tree branch in the shade, where there was a strange object already hanging from a hook.

'What on earth's that thing?' whispered James, eyeing the contraption that seemed to be a tube made of wire and old net curtain. It was gathered at the top and bottom and there was a plastic plate in the base.

'I think it's a food safe,' Mandy said. 'It keeps food cool and stops flies getting on to it. I saw instructions on how to make one in an old Girl Guides book of Mum's.'

'I didn't know people still made stuff like that,' said James.

'It looks like Flora does!'

Half an hour later, James jumped up. He and Mandy had been enjoying throwing a hard rubber ball for Sparky. 'What time is it? I've just remembered I've got to get back early. Mum's visitor's staying to tea.' He looked really guilty.

'Oh, dear,' Flora said, looking concerned. 'Have Sparky and I kept you from something important?'

'No. I mean yes. Well – sort of,' James stammered, blushing. 'But it's not your fault.'

Mandy turned to James. 'It isn't very late. If we leave right now and get a move on we'll reach your house in plenty of time.'

'OK.' James looked relieved.

As they reached the gate they waved goodbye. 'Bye! Flora. Thanks for the tea. Bye, Sparky.' Flora was piling fruit into the food safe. She looked over her shoulder and waved back.

'See you again, I hope. I'll probably camp here on my way back in a few days' time.' Abruptly, she turned away and crawled into the low opening of her tent. They heard her say, 'Now, Sparky, which side do you want your sleeping bag?'

'I bet she made Sparky's bed herself as well!' James said as they walked their bikes along the outside of the new fence. 'Flora's really wacky, isn't she?'

'Wacky but nice,' Mandy said firmly.

'That's what I meant!' James said with a chuckle. Mandy laughed too.

They threw themselves on to their bikes. 'Race you,' James called, speeding out of the gate.

'OK. You're on!' Mandy flew after him, down the side of the campsite fence.

As Wilfred's cottage whizzed by, Mandy glanced at it, tempted to slow down. But in that brief second, she saw that there was no sign of movement at the windows and the front door was firmly closed. No sign of Wilfred sunning himself in the doorway.

The little nagging feeling was still there inside her. Despite James's words earlier it wouldn't go away. Mandy's instincts still told her that something just wasn't right.

The sound of Mr Hope's rich baritone voice echoed around the sitting room. He was singing hymns, rehearsing for choir practice. The smell of baked potatoes filled the cottage. Supper would soon be ready, but Mandy wanted a word with her dad before they sat down to eat.

She slipped quietly in through the door and curled up on the sofa. The sitting room was cosy, with its low ceiling and wooden beams. Red patterned rugs covered the stone floor. In the winter a log fire burned in the inglenook fireplace, but right now the space was filled by a copper bucket packed to bursting with wallflowers from Grandad's garden.

Mr Hope sang on, while Mandy leafed through an old copy of *The Dalesman*. He tailed off after a few moments.

'Interesting read?' he said innocently.

Mandy grinned and put down the magazine. 'Not really.'

'OK. Out with it then,' her dad said. 'I know that look. You're hatching something.'

Mandy told her dad about the events of the day. 'We didn't see Wilfred,' she explained. 'I wondered if you'd mind phoning him.'

'Still worried about him, are you?'

She nodded. 'He's just not himself, Dad.'

'Of course he's not. His wife's just died, Mandy,' Adam Hope said gently.

Mandy bit her lip. 'Yes, I know. Do you think that's why he won't talk about Matty?'

'Ah, Matty. Of course!' Her dad closed his song book. 'OK, love. I'll give Wilfred a ring. I've been meaning to check that he's OK anyway.'

'Thanks, Dad!' Mandy jumped up. 'I'll go and help Mum with the supper.'

A few minutes later, Mr Hope came into the kitchen. Mandy was grating cheese into a bowl. Her dad took a pinch of cheese and popped it into his mouth. Mandy paused, too impatient for news of Wilfred to scold him.

'Did you speak to Wilfred, Adam?' Emily Hope asked, setting out plates.

'Yes,' Mr Hope said. 'He sounds fine, says he's coping well by himself.'

'Did you ask him about Matty?' Mandy asked eagerly. 'Is she settling in OK? Are her new owners nearby?'

'Whoa! One question at a time!' her dad replied with a grin. 'I mentioned Matty. Wilfred said I'm not to worry about her. Everything's fine. He said he'll explain next time he sees me.'

'But what does that mean?' Mandy persisted.

'It means that this food is ready,' her mum said firmly. 'Would you bring that bowl of salad over please, Mandy?'

As she took her place at the table, Mandy was thoughtful. She seemed to be the only one who thought there was something strange about this whole thing. Could she be wrong? As she cut open a baked potato and mashed butter into it, she caught her dad's eye.

'Don't worry, love,' Mr Hope said. 'It's understandable that Wilfred wants to be left alone after what he's been through.'

'Yes,' Mrs Hope agreed. 'And we must respect his wishes, Mandy. All right?'

'All right,' Mandy said reluctantly. But it wasn't all right. And it wouldn't be until she knew for certain where Matty was.

Four

Emily Hope popped a worming tablet into a small envelope. 'If you're going round to Gran and Grandad's, you may as well take this for Smoky,' she said to Mandy.

Smoky was Mandy's gran and grandad's adopted cat.

'OK,' Mandy said, slipping the envelope into her jeans pocket.

Her mum wore a dark green suit with a cream blouse underneath, and her red hair was tied back. She was speaking at a veterinary conference near York and staying for the dinner afterwards.

'You look really nice, Mum. I hope the talk goes well.'

As Mrs Hope smiled, the freckles seemed to dance

on her cheeks. 'Thanks, love. Ah, that sounds like my lift.' She reached for her handbag and folder. 'See you later.'

'Bye!' Mandy called.

Saturdays were short working days at the practice. With her mum out all day, Simon, the practice nurse, would be helping her dad with morning surgery. Mr Hope would be doing the calls after surgery finished. Simon was just arriving as Mandy closed the cottage door behind her: a tall, thin figure, with newly-cut fair hair and spectacles. He raised his hand in a cheery wave.

Most of the school holiday was gone already, Mandy thought, as she walked up the lane. She felt restless and a bit edgy. If only she knew where Matty was. Thoughts of the little silver-grey mare continued to niggle at her, but as no one else seemed concerned she had decided to keep her worries to herself.

A sigh escaped her. She told herself that a visit to her grandparents was just what she needed. There was always something going on at Lilac Cottage.

Just then she saw her dad returning to Animal Ark in the Land-rover. He had been out to Woodbridge Farm Park on the Walton Road.

Mr Hope pulled up beside the grass verge and

leaned across to the open window. 'Hello, love. Where are you off to?'

'I'm meeting James and Blackie at Gran's,' she replied. 'We thought we might help out in the garden.'

'It's a nice thought. Your grandad swears that weeds grow overnight at this time of year,' Mr Hope chuckled. 'But I'm not sure that Blackie and the word "help" go together!'

Mandy smiled 'Was there a serious problem at the Farm Park, Dad?'

'No. Just routine inoculations, then Mr Marsh asked me to check over four new arrivals.'

'What were they?' Mandy asked. 'Anything interesting?'

'I thought all animals were interesting to you!'

'Of course they are! You know what I mean.'

He nodded, his mild blue eyes teasing. 'Actually – these *are* a bit unusual. Mr Marsh thinks his customers might find them interesting. They're Soay sheep; four of them.'

'Oh. What are they like?'

'Small, brownish, with tiny little horns,' Mr Hope said. 'They're an ancient breed, very tough and quite rare now.'

'They sound lovely,' Mandy breathed. 'Can I go and see them sometime?'

Her dad flashed her a grin. 'Now how did I know you were going to say that? I've got to call back there in a day or two. You can come with me if you like.'

'Great!'

He moved the Land-rover forwards. 'Got to go and see a man about a dog! Bye, love! Say hello to your gran and grandad for me.'

Mandy waved. 'I will!' she called, as she continued on up the lane.

She reached the gate, with its Lilac Cottage sign, just as James arrived. His head appeared, bobbing over the top of the neatly trimmed hedges.

'Hi, James. Hi, Blackie.'

The Labrador gave a friendly woof and wagged his tail as Mandy patted his head.

The bushes that gave the cottage its name were in full bloom, and a strong sweet scent hung on the air. Mandy and James had reached the front door, when they caught sight of a movement in the camper van parked on the side drive.

First a hand appeared, scrubbing briskly away at the window with a piece of damp, crumpled newspaper. Then a face, topped by neat grey hair, came into view.

'Hi, Gran!' Mandy waved.

Her gran waved back. She was wearing a checked

apron and bright pink rubber gloves – just like an advert for washing-up liquid.

'What's she doing with that newspaper?' asked James.

'It's probably one of her short-cuts,' Mandy replied. Her gran was a mine of information about such things. 'She says she's going to write a book one day – called, "1001 Things to Do Around the House with Vinegar",' Mandy said.

'Vinegar! Was she joking?'

Mandy grinned. 'Probably, but I'm not sure!'

James shook his head in disbelief, his dark fringe flopping about. 'She ought to get on well with Flora Pearson!'

'Mandy, love!' Gran's face lit up as she came out of the camper van to meet them. She placed a plastic bowl on the ground. It was full of cleaning things: dusters, polish, scouring pads – and a bottle of vinegar. 'How's my favourite granddaughter?'

Mandy almost spluttered with laughter as she saw James looking suspiciously at the bottle of vinegar. 'Your *only* granddaughter is fine, thanks very much!' she managed to say.

'Hello, James,' Mrs Hope's wide smile shone on James too. Stripping off the apron and rubber gloves, she bent to give Blackie a pat.

'Hello, Mrs Hope,' said James.

Mandy took the small envelope out of her pocket. 'Mum sent you this, for Smoky.'

'Thanks, love.' Gran put the worming tablet in her dress pocket.

'You look busy,' Mandy said. 'Are you spring-cleaning the camper?'

Gran's eyes twinkled. 'You could call it that.'

'What do you mean?' asked Mandy puzzled.

'I've been keeping out of the way.'

'Why?' Mandy asked.

'Come over here and see,' Gran said mysteriously.

Mandy, James, and Blackie wandered across to the garden. There were fruit trees and bushes, rows of peas and beans, bushy potato plants on top of ridges, brightly coloured flowers bursting from their beds. Every inch of soil had been planted. Nothing could resist Grandad's green fingers.

The greenhouse backed up to the garden fence. In the narrow space behind it, they saw Mandy's grandad and a small man with grizzled whitish hair. Both men had a firm hold of the same panel of fencing.

'That's Ernie Bell with Grandad,' Mandy said, surprised.

Ernie Bell was a retired carpenter. He lived in a tiny cottage behind the Fox and Goose. He was grumpy and stubborn, but Mandy knew that his unfriendly scowl hid a good heart.

Gran nodded, looking rather pleased with herself. 'Yes. Your grandad was struggling with taking down that damaged fence panel when Ernie just happened to call by and offer to help.'

Mandy chuckled. 'Oh, he did, did he? What have you been up to, Gran?'

Gran smiled and reached up to sweep some stray hairs back into the pleat at the back of her head. 'I only mentioned to Ernie that your Grandad couldn't really manage the fence alone. I told him that he needed help with the repairs, but was too proud to ask for it.'

'Gran! You are awful,' Mandy said.

'I know. But it worked. Ernie couldn't resist calling round to have a look, being a retired carpenter. I knew he'd be dying to lend a hand, but it's no good asking him outright. You have to know how to handle him.'

Mandy nodded. 'We know! He loves helping really, but he has to do things his own way.'

'Like when he made that pen for Lucky,' put in James. Lucky was a little fox cub Mandy and James had once rescued.

'But why have you been keeping out of the way in the camper?' Mandy asked.

Gran gave another of her twinkling grins. 'Ernie's getting a bit wise to my tricks. I thought I'd let your Grandad handle things this time. Just look at him! How do you think he's doing?'

Grandad and Ernie seemed to be engaged in some kind of comical dance. They were jigging back and forth, pulling at the fence, bending to get a better grip. Then they stopped altogether and stood back to weigh things up. Grandad scratched his head. Ernie Bell rubbed the grey whiskers on his jutting chin.

'I only hope Ernie doesn't keep calling your grandad, "young Tom",' whispered Gran.

Mandy, James, and Gran stood there watching. Next to little old Ernie, Mandy's grandad looked tall and straight. At sixty-five, he was as fit as a flea. He was always on the go: gardening, walking, cycling.

'Dear me. I seem to be making a right hash of this,' Grandad said. 'It's a good thing you're here, Ernie.'

Good for you, Grandad, Mandy thought.

'Out of the way,' Ernie said, puffing up his chest. 'Let me get a look at it.'

Grandad moved aside.

'Now then, young Tom. Grab a hold,' Ernie ordered. 'That's it. Give it a heave and it'll come free of those rusty nails.'

'Right you are,' Grandad said meekly, on his best behaviour. 'You're the expert. Best retired carpenter in Yorkshire. No one better.'

Mandy cringed. *Don't overdo it, Grandad!*

Ernie frowned. 'Humph! Don't know about that,' he muttered grumpily, but he looked pleased.

Mandy breathed a sigh of relief. Ernie was falling for it.

'Now,' Ernie said, fully in charge now. 'One, two, three – lift!'

With a final heave and a screech of metal the fence panel came loose. Grandad and Ernie edged sideways, crab fashion. Moments later the damaged panel was propped against the wooden upright.

'Phew!' Grandad dusted off his hands. He looked up and waved. 'Hello there. We seem to have attracted quite an audience!'

Mandy and James waved back. 'Hi, Grandad,' called Mandy. 'Hello, Mr Bell! How's Sammy?'

'He's grand, thanks,' Ernie Bell's wrinkled, weather-beaten face relaxed into a grin. 'Bright eyed and bushy tailed!' He could never resist talking about his pet squirrel. He had brought Sammy into Animal Ark after his mother was run over.

'Tea up in five minutes,' Gran said.

'Right,' Grandad said, turning back to the fence panel.

The high winds of winter had torn ragged holes and splintered the wood. It was a complete mess. Mandy saw her grandad scratch his head.

'Thanks for your help, Ernie. I expect I'd better have a go at patching this up now,' he said doubtfully.

'Patch it up!' Ernie Bell's face wore a look of disgust. 'I don't patch things up. I do a proper job or I don't do it all. Out of the way, Tom. Let me have a look.' He fished in his trousers pocket and took out a tape measure.

Grandad moved nimbly aside. 'You just tell me what I need and I'll go and get it from Fenton's timberyard.'

'No need for that,' Ernie said, putting his head on one side. 'I've got to pick up my tools. I'll collect what we need on the way. Now have you got any nails? It's important to have the right size . . .'

Grandad winked at Mandy as he and Ernie moved towards the small garden shed. She smiled back at him. *Well done*!

In the spotless kitchen, Gran made tea and poured glasses of home-made lemonade for Mandy and James. She had been baking that morning and the whole cottage smelt wonderful. On the table there was a pie, a crispy lattice-work of pastry covering the fruit.

'Mmmm. What is it?' Mandy asked. 'Apple and blackberries from your freezer?'

'Extra insurance!' Gran said, with a wicked smile. 'Just in case Ernie needed more persuading.'

'Don't you mean bribing?' Mandy said.

'Mandy Hope! The very idea,' Gran teased. She cut thick slices and placed them on plates, then said to Mandy, 'Would you fetch me the ice-cream from the freezer, love?'

Mandy washed her hands and helped Gran dole out scoops of vanilla ice-cream. Just then, Smoky came into the kitchen. Blackie sidled up to the cat in a friendly fashion, his tail wagging back and forth.

Mandy bent down to stroke the cat's silky grey fur. Smoky purred, twining around Mandy's legs. Then he sniffed at her hand and began licking her fingers. Mandy giggled as the cat's warm, rough tongue tickled.

'It must be the ice-cream!' said James. He chuckled. 'I bet Sparky likes ice-cream too.'

'Bound to. I bet he even eats it with his own special spoon!' Mandy joked.

'Who's Sparky?' Gran said suspiciously. 'Not another of your waifs and strays needing a good home?'

'Not this time!' Mandy said. 'Sparky belongs to Flora Pearson, someone we met up at Western's

Campsite.' She and James filled her in on all the details about the eccentric woman and her quirky pet. '. . . and Flora's coming back this way, so we'll probably get to see her and Sparky up at the campsite again,' she finished.

Gran smiled. 'They sound like a colourful pair!'

'They are,' agreed James.

'What's that?' Ernie Bell said, coming into the kitchen with Grandad. On Gran's invitation, he took a seat at the table. 'Did somebody mention campers?'

Mandy nodded. 'We were just telling Gran about someone we met up at Western's Campsite the other day.'

Ernie gave a dry chuckle that sounded like a rusty door creaking open. 'Huh! Sam Western's not having things all his own way,' he said. 'Been a bit of a to-do up there by all accounts.'

'What sort of a to-do?' asked Grandad.

But Ernie seemed in no hurry to share his juicy gossip. He sipped his tea and chewed slowly on a big wedge of pie and ice-cream.

'Another slice, Ernie?' Gran asked sweetly.

'Don't mind if I do – if it's going begging,' Ernie said, somehow managing to sound as if he was doing Gran a favour.

Mandy and James were almost fidgeting with

impatience. If something was going on up at the new campsite they definitely wanted to know about it! At long last, Ernie pushed his empty plate away. He looked around the table, enjoying having a captive audience.

'That there campsite's haunted,' he stated, matter-of-factly.

Mandy and James blinked at him. Gran looked indignant. It was plain that she didn't believe it – not for one minute. She opened her mouth to speak, but Grandad laid a hand on her arm. 'What makes you say that?' he asked mildly.

'It's not me saying it,' Ernie said. 'It's the campers. Leastways, according to Mrs McFarlane.'

'Mrs McFarlane!' Gran said, with a sniff. 'If a leaf fell in the woods that woman would hear it!'

Ernie looked put out. 'Well, if you don't want to know what I've got say . . .' he said huffily, half-rising from the table.

'We want to know, don't we, James?' Mandy burst out.

James nodded.

'Go on then, Ernie,' Grandad said. 'Let's hear the rest of it.'

Ernie sank back into his chair. 'Well – as I heard it, a couple of campers called into the post office on their way out of Welford. Said they'd had just about enough and they'd decided to pack up and move on.'

'But why?' asked Mandy.

'Because of them funny goings on,' Ernie said darkly.

Mandy leaned forward eagerly, her blue eyes wide. 'What sort of goings on?'

'Ghostly ones,' Ernie said, deadly serious. 'People have heard hoof beats on the road beyond the fence. And . . .' he leaned forward, his face intent, '. . . someone saw a headless horseman, riding by on a ghost horse.'

Mandy's mouth dropped open. She looked across at James.

'Stuff and nonsense!' Gran said, in her usual practical way. 'I don't take kindly to you frightening my granddaughter with these silly stories, Ernie Bell.'

'Oh, it takes more than that to rattle Mandy,' said Grandad. 'She's got a level head on her shoulders.'

'Oh-argh. Stories, is it?' Ernie said, dropping his voice to a gruff whisper. 'Then why's the campsite half-empty, eh? Tell me that. Something's definitely putting people off camping up there.'

'But a headless horseman . . .' Grandad said reasonably.

Ernie looked a bit sheepish. 'Well – maybe not headless,' he admitted. 'But the rest of it's true. One of the campers told the McFarlanes how he looked out of his tent in the dead of night and he saw it – the outline of a man on a horse. All misty and shadowy it was.'

Mandy felt a shiver run down her spine. She didn't know whether to feel frightened or fascinated by Ernie's spooky stories. They couldn't be true. Could they? James glanced at her and she knew he felt the same.

'Well – I don't know what to make of this at all,' Gran said. 'It sounds very far fetched.'

Ernie gave another of his rusty laughs. 'Even if it is, there's one good thing about it!'

'What's that?' asked Mandy a bit nervously.

'Sam Western's going to be hopping mad! With the field half-empty he'll lose money. Serve him right. I never liked the idea of him doing well out of old Wilfred Bennett's misfortunes!'

'I won't argue with that,' said Grandad.

'Hee-hee,' Ernie chuckled. 'There's nothing Sam Western can do about a ghost!'

'Well,' Gran said thoughtfully, 'I'm not saying I believe a word of all this. But there's no smoke without fire.'

Five

Mandy and James paused by the village green, Ernie Bell's creepy stories still on their minds.

Suddenly, James waved his arms about and made loud 'Woo-oo! Woo-oo!' noises. Then he rolled his eyes, gave a strangled groan and sank on to the grass beneath the huge oak tree. Blackie capered around him, wagging his tail and licking his face.

'Don't!' Mandy fell about laughing. She couldn't think of a less frightening ghost – and Blackie was making enough racket to see off a whole number of spooks!

'Do you think it's true about the ghostly horse and rider?' James said, on his feet once again and brushing at the grass seeds sticking to his sweater.

'*Headless* rider!' Mandy said, still chuckling. 'Get it right!'

'Didn't your gran say Ernie's been taking a leaf out of your book?' James asked with a cheeky grin.

Mandy felt herself going a bit pink, but she had to laugh. She knew she had a tendency to exaggerate. 'Well, anyway, Grandad says the whole story's probably just a load of nonsense.'

James shrugged. 'Do you agree with him?'

'I don't know. But there's one sure way to find out!'

'Go up there, you mean?' James looked rather alarmed.

'Yep. I'm game if you are. What do you say?'

James put his head on one side. 'Well – OK,' he said uncertainly. 'Course it would be no good going in the daytime.'

'No,' agreed Mandy. 'The ghostly horseman is only seen at night. We'd have to be up there quite late . . .' Suddenly she saw problems looming. 'What would we tell our parents?'

James screwed up his face, thinking hard. Suddenly he wagged his finger. 'Hang on! I've got it – badgers!'

Mandy looked at him. 'What have badgers got to do with this?'

'We could ask permission to do a badger watch.

The new sett's up by the campsite, so it would almost be true.'

'That's a brilliant idea!'

'Here you are, love,' Mr Hope said that evening. 'You can borrow these binoculars. They have special infra-red night vision.'

'Thanks, Dad.' Mandy felt a bit guilty as she promised to take good care of them.

'Hang on.' Her dad was in full flow, enthusiastic and helpful. 'There won't be much of a moon. You'd better take this torch as well. It's dark in those woods.'

'OK.' Mandy thrust the binoculars and torch into a hold-all and slung it over her shoulder.

Mr Hope began to sing, his rich voice swelling in the room. 'Oh, Mandy went out one moonlit night . . .'

Mandy ducked and hurried towards the door. Her dad could be so embarrassing sometimes.

'. . . she prayed for the moon to give her light. For she had many a mile to go that night. Before she reached the town-o—' Her dad stopped abruptly and sang out, 'Happy brock-watching!'

'Thanks!' she called out. 'We'll make sure we're back just after ten.'

It was just getting dark when she met James at the

crossroads. Bats were swooping low over the trees and the hollow hoot of an owl echoed across the fields. The moon had risen: a thin slice, like a nail paring.

James's eyes lit up behind his glasses when he looked through the binoculars. 'Wow! Just what we need for ghost-busting!'

They pedalled hard to the edge of the village, but slowed down on the unlit winding bends. Soon Wilfred Bennett's cottage came into view. There was a light in the kitchen window, but the rest of the cottage was in darkness. Mandy felt a pang at the thought of the old man in there all alone.

They brought their bikes to a halt outside the campsite. The big wooden fence looked black against a dark blue sky that was pricked by stars. Wind rustled in the trees, and from far off there came the strange, coughing bark of a vixen. Suddenly it didn't seem like such a good idea to be up here by themselves. It was easy to imagine that a ghostly horseman would come sailing through the hedgerow.

'What's the plan?' asked James, squaring his shoulders.

Mandy knew he was nervous, but trying to hide it. 'Let's put our bikes in the camping field. Then we can have a scout around.'

'Fine by me.'

Mandy peered into the darkness as she wheeled her bike in through the gate and leaned it against a tree. She stood looking around. A faint light came from the old stable block, way off across the field. It made a dull beacon in a sea of darkness.

'There aren't many tents in here,' said James, his voice sounding a bit wobbly. 'It's a bit creepy, isn't it?'

Mandy usually reckoned that her nerves were as strong as steel. In the surgery she had seen her parents give blood transfusions, operate on stomachs, and sew up wounds. But ghosts were another thing entirely.

'Maybe a bit,' she said, trying to put on a brave face.

Suddenly James tensed. 'What was that?'

Mandy jumped. 'What?'

'I thought I heard something,' James said. 'Out on the road . . .'

Mandy listened hard, but could hear nothing. 'What kind of noise was it?'

'I don't know. Sort of like . . . clopping . . . It's stopped now.'

Mandy gulped. 'The ghost!' She dug in her hold-all for the torch as she went for the gate at a run.

'Wait for me!' James sprang after her.

Suddenly, yapping like fury, a small dog streaked down the field and hurtled past them.

'Oh!' Mandy faltered and lost her grip on the torch. The dog had brushed past her legs, dashing towards the open gate. She recognised that brown and white shape. Sparky!

Recovering her stride, Mandy raced after the dog, reaching the gateway just in time to see a car's headlights sweep the grass verge in a wide arc. Still barking, Sparky leapt out into the road, straight into the path of the car.

'Look out!' Mandy screamed.

Too late. Car brakes screeched. There was a bang and a yelp of pain.

'Oh, no!'

Ghostly horsemen, strange noises, everything was forgotten as Mandy rushed towards a real-life emergency. The car had skidded across the road. As it drew to a halt, the driver emerged. He was a stocky, balding man in a dark suit. Shakily he walked over to Mandy and James, who had gone straight to Sparky. He bent down and peered at the little dog as it lay on its side in the road.

'Oh, Lord. This is terrible,' he stammered, looking up as Mandy threw herself to her knees beside the injured animal. 'I swerved, but I couldn't miss it. Is it your dog?'

Mandy shook her head, gulping back tears, as she reached out towards the little brown and white animal. 'No. But I know him. His name's Sparky.'

Although her hands shook, she felt herself grow calm. She had to help Sparky. The little dog's eyes opened briefly as she knelt beside him. Mandy spoke to him in a soothing, comforting voice. She knew that talking gently to hurt animals calmed them. It helped to keep their pulses steady if they were in shock.

Quickly she checked the dog's breathing. He was panting hard and there was a lot of blood on his back leg.

'Sparky! Oh, no!' Flora Pearson ran up to the little group huddled round her dog. She wrung her hands. Tears glistened on her cheeks. 'The silly boy! He dashed out of the tent before I could stop him. It was the sound of hoof beats. He can't abide horses.'

Without her red beret Flora's hair stuck out in wispy strands. She wore a baggy orange T-shirt, with 'Save the Whales' printed on it in large letters.

'Mandy knows what to do,' James said. 'Don't worry.'

'Oh, yes. Mandy's the local vets' daughter, isn't she?' Flora said, scrubbing at her eyes.

'It's going to be all right, Sparky,' Mandy said softly.

The injured leg was bleeding badly. Somehow she had to try and stop the flow, but how? Then she remembered helping her mum treat a vixen which had been caught in a trap. Hurriedly she took a clean handkerchief out of her jeans pocket and tied it tightly around Sparky's leg in a make-shift bandage.

'There now, boy,' she murmured as Sparky whimpered in pain.

The little dog turned his head. Mandy moved slowly and carefully; injured animals could snap. But Sparky only licked her hand feebly. He seemed grateful for her help.

'That'll help stop the bleeding,' Mandy said. 'But we have to take it off soon. The leg needs proper treatment.' She wished her mum or dad were there. Sparky needed expert care, and quickly.

The motorist had been silent up to now. He still looked shaken. 'Can I do anything?'

'Yes,' Mandy said. 'Can you drive us to Animal Ark, please? That's my parents' surgery.'

'Right.' The man, who introduced himself as Bob Foster, took off his jacket. He spread it out. 'You can use this as a stretcher.'

Gently, with Flora's help, Mandy laid Sparky on top. Then everyone piled into the car.

*   *   *

Mr Hope took one look at Mandy's flushed face and took charge. 'Bring him straight through to the treatment room,' he said. 'Mandy – I'll need your help. Would everyone else wait here, please?'

Mandy watched her dad scrub up and put on rubber gloves. 'You did well, Mandy,' he said over his shoulder. 'That bandage certainly slowed the bleeding.'

She held Sparky gently while her dad checked him over thoroughly, searching with his quick, practised fingers.

'No internal injuries,' Mr Hope said after a while. 'But that leg has a bad break. It could need an operation.' He gave the little dog an injection and sedated him. 'We'll need to do an X-ray, but I suspect that bone will have to be pinned.'

Mandy frowned with concern. 'Will the leg heal properly?'

'Should do,' Mr Hope said confidently. 'Jack Russells are tough little things.'

Mandy breathed a huge sigh of relief. She helped make Sparky comfortable in a large cage in the residential unit. When she left, the little dog had settled down with his nose between his paws.

'Have a good rest,' she said as she left. 'You've been very brave.'

As Mandy and her dad came out into the waiting room, she heard Flora talking to Bob Foster. Bob was insisting on paying for Sparky's treatment.

'Whatever it costs,' he said. 'Poor little tyke.'

'Very well. If you insist. That's most kind.' Flora's voice was firm, despite her upset. She managed to look dignified in her baggy shorts and bright orange T-shirt. 'But you really mustn't blame yourself. Once he heard those hoof beats, nothing could stop him . . .'

Mandy was suddenly alert. That was the second time Flora had mentioned hoof beats. And James had thought he heard a sound on the road, just before Sparky ran out. She was dying to ask Flora some questions, but now wasn't the time.

Catching sight of Mr Hope, Flora paused; her thin face looked pale and strained. 'How is he?'

Mandy's dad smiled. 'Resting comfortably now. I'll need to check the X-rays before I treat that leg. I'll do it first thing in the morning.'

Flora lifted her chin. 'Thank you,' she said. She turned to Mandy. 'And thank you. I don't know what I'd have done if . . .'

'That's OK,' Mandy said hurriedly. She always got embarrassed when people thanked her.

Bob offered to give Flora a lift back to the campsite and drop James home on the way. 'Oh,'

James said, remembering. 'We've left our bikes in the field.'

'Oh, no! I've left my hold-all too,' Mandy said. 'I must have dropped it inside the gate.' She looked up at her dad guiltily. His torch and binoculars were inside it. 'Sorry, Dad.'

'That's all right, love.' Mr Hope ruffled his daughter's fair hair. 'You had other things on your mind.'

Flora promised to look after the hold-all and bikes, and Mandy and James arranged to go and collect them the following day.

'It's a bit late to go back up there now,' Mr Hope agreed, as he saw everyone to the door. When they had gone, he turned to Mandy. 'One thing puzzles me.'

'What's that, Dad?' Mandy said, sidling towards the stairs, her blue eyes wide.

He lifted one dark eyebrow. 'How many badgers were you expecting to see at the campsite?'

Mumbling about 'a short cut up to the woods', Mandy made a dash for the stairs. Over her shoulder she saw that her dad was staring after her, a quizzical look on his face.

Just then there was the sound of a vehicle on the drive. The front door opened and Emily Hope came in, looking tired. 'Hi, everyone. I'm home!'

Adam Hope greeted his wife warmly. 'How did it go?'

'It was a long day.' Mrs Hope smiled. 'The conference was fine. The dinner was . . . interesting!'

'We've had an interesting evening too. Haven't we, Mandy?'

Mandy came downstairs to hug her mum briefly. 'You tell Mum all about it, Dad. I'm bushed!' she said, pleading tiredness, and dashed up to her bedroom.

Phew! she thought. *One lucky escape*!

Six

Flora Pearson was sitting outside her tent when Mandy and James arrived early on Sunday morning. She was drinking tea out of one of her bright tin mugs. Sparky's empty yellow mug sat on the grass to one side.

'How's Sparky?' asked Flora at once, pouring tea for Mandy and James.

'He's doing fine,' Mandy said. 'Dad didn't have to operate, after all.'

Flora nodded her head, the red beret bobbing. 'But the leg was broken?'

Mandy nodded. 'Dad said it was a clean break. He's set it and put a special plastic bandage on it.'

'Oh, dear. Poor Sparky.'

'It'll be all right,' James said encouragingly.

'Mandy's mum and dad are brilliant vets.'

Flora's sudden grin enlivened her thin face. 'Their daughter's pretty clever too!'

Mandy didn't think she was clever. She had just done what needed doing. She was especially sensitive about road accidents because her own parents had been killed in a car crash. Adam and Emily Hope had adopted her when she was a baby and now they were as real as any mum and dad could be.

'Dad says Sparky can come back up here tomorrow,' Mandy said. 'But he told me to tell you he wants to check to see if the leg is healing properly in a few days' time.'

'Oh, that's fine. I'll make sure he gets lots of rest. I shall be staying on the site until he's completely recovered. No more fell-walking for a while!' She puffed out her bony chest, clad this morning in a lime green T-shirt with the motto 'Animal Power' embroidered across it. 'It'll take more than a night apparition to make me move on without my Sparky!'

'Dad said not to worry. He'll bring Sparky back up here in the Land-rover . . .' Mandy suddenly realised what Flora had said. She gasped. 'You saw the ghostly horseman?'

'Oh, yes,' Flora said, as if it was the most normal thing in the world. 'Sparky and I were coming back from the Fox and Goose, the night before last, when it appeared out of the mist.' She chuckled. 'I don't know who was more shocked, me or the phantom!'

'Wow!' James looked at Mandy, then back at Flora. 'What did it look like?'

'All sort of pale and glowing – a horse and rider. I caught just a shadowy glimpse, then Sparky went into a frenzy, pulling at his lead and growling. I had the dickens of a job trying to control him. By the time I looked up again – the ghost had gone.'

'Weren't you scared?' Mandy asked.

Flora looked thoughtful for a moment, then she shook her head. 'Not really. I know it sounds strange, but I had the feeling that it was more scared of me. It certainly cleared off sharp enough!'

Mandy and James sat in stunned silence as they finished their tea.

'And you think it came back, last night?' Mandy asked at last.

'When you were inside your tent?' put in James.

'Yes,' Flora agreed. 'This time, Sparky didn't wait to see it. As soon as he heard that clip-clopping outside the fence, he was up and out of the tent opening before I could grab him.'

James gave a sudden shiver. 'I think I might have heard it too!' His voice sounded funny.

Mandy frowned. It was hard to believe in ghosts, but Flora had definitely seen something. A horse and rider, she had said. But there were no horses stabled around here any more. Mandy didn't know what to think.

A short while later, Flora fetched Mandy's hold-all from her tent. 'Here you are, my dear. And your bikes are tied to the tree. I'll come and help you undo the knots.'

Mandy and James watched in astonishment as Flora took hold of the complicated-looking knots and untied them with a flourish. 'There. Nothing to it. I always could tie a ripping sheepshank!'

Flora decided to walk into Welford with them, as she wanted to visit Sparky. 'I'll take him a bit of my flapjack. That'll cheer him up.'

Mandy grinned at James. They were both thinking the same thing. Good job she wasn't going to take his yellow mug and brew up in the Animal Ark kitchen!

Outside the campsite, Mandy and James wheeled their bikes along beside Flora. Mandy glanced towards Wilfred's cottage as they passed by. Once again there was no sign of their friend.

Flora swung her arms, striding out along the Welford Road. They soon reached the village. At the top of the lane Mandy and James paused.

'Animal Ark's just down there,' Mandy said, pointing. 'You can't miss it.'

'Thanks. Everything looks so different in the daylight.' Flora's face clouded as she remembered last night's harrowing journey in Bob Foster's car.

'Sparky had a lucky escape,' Mandy said.

'Yes.' Flora's face brightened. She waved goodbye as Mandy and James got on their bikes. 'See you soon I expect!'

It was James's idea to call into the post office, before the bike ride to school the following morning. He wanted to buy crisps. Mandy was at the counter paying for her favourite treat, sherbet, when the doorbell rang and Ernie Bell came into the shop.

'Hi, Mr Bell,' they chorused.

'Now then, you two,' Ernie replied, a smile flickering across his grumpy face. He took a newspaper from the stand and nodded a greeting to Mrs McFarlane, who was replacing the big glass jar of rainbow-striped sherbet on its shelf.

'Morning, Ernie,' Mrs McFarlane said, ringing money into the till. Her round face lit up. 'Have you heard the latest? The ghostly horseman was heard again last night. A little dog ran after it and got knocked down by a car. The whole village's buzzing with it.'

Mandy looked at Mrs McFarlane in surprise. How had word spread so quickly?

'You two were up there, weren't you?' said the postmistress. 'Lucky for that poor dog. Did either of you see the ghost?'

Mandy shook her head and James did the same. It was best to say nothing. Her gran said Mrs McFarlane had a gift for making mountains out of molehills.

'Have you heard anything, Mr Bell?' Mrs McFarlane asked.

Ernie stroked his grizzled chin and developed a sudden marked interest in the display of chocolate bars on the counter. James and Mandy exchanged glances. They knew Ernie loved a good gossip just as much as Mrs McFarlane, but sometimes he liked to pretend he was above such things.

'Anything at all . . .?' the postmistress encouraged.

'We-ell,' Ernie began grudgingly. 'I did hear that Sam Western's hopping mad about the whole thing.' He gave one of his surprising rusty chuckles. 'Carryin' on something dreadful he were, apparently, saying that all this ghostie rubbish is ruining his business.'

Mrs McFarlane's eyes crinkled. She crossed her arms and hitched her bosom up with a twitch of her elbows. 'It doesn't take much for that man to start lording it about,' she said with a disapproving sniff. 'He thinks he can snap his fingers and everyone will jump to his tune.'

'You're right there,' agreed Ernie. 'Western's even got Dennis Saville looking into things for him.'

'Hmmph!' snorted Mrs McFarlane. 'That one! He needs a personality transplant.'

Mandy and James looked at each other, trying not to laugh. For once they agreed with her.

'Saville won't have much luck,' commented Ernie, his head on one side. 'You can't stop folk talking. No matter how much you try.'

Ernie paid for his newspaper and bought a bag of monkey nuts for Sammy, his pet squirrel. He pocketed his change and turned to go. At the door he waved to Mandy and James.

'I'm just off to Lilac Cottage to finish that fence panel. Young Tom's got no idea about carpentry. No idea at all.'

The bell clanged as the door closed, and Mandy and James burst out laughing.

'What?' Mrs McFarlane said, her nose in the air like a bloodhound scenting a fresh trail. 'Is it a private joke or can anyone join in?'

Still chuckling, Mandy and James made a grab for the door.

'Well – what do you think?' Grandad said, his arms spread wide in front of the new fence panel. 'Counter-sunk screws and everything!'

'A perfect job!' Mandy said with a grin. It was a lovely clear evening; she and James had come round to Lilac Cottage for tea, after a busy day at school.

'You have to give it to Ernie,' her gran said. 'He's difficult and crotchety, but he knows his stuff.'

'He does that,' Grandad said. 'He huffed and puffed a bit, but I caught him smiling when he thought I wasn't looking. He really enjoyed showing me the ropes!'

They all chuckled.

'I hear you two have been busy too,' Gran said. 'How's that little dog?'

Mandy told her that Sparky was doing well. 'He managed to limp a few steps this morning. Dad's surprised how well he's doing.'

'The accident must have happened almost outside Wilfred Bennett's cottage,' Gran said thoughtfully.

'Yes, it did,' said James. 'Just metres away.'

'You didn't happen to see any sign of Wilfred, did you?' asked Gran, glancing meaningfully at her husband.

'No.' Mandy saw the look. 'We've been up near his cottage a couple of times, but we haven't seen him. Why?'

'Your gran's getting a bit worried about the old chap,' Grandad said.

'It's just that no one in the village has seen Wilfred for ages,' Gran said. 'I was going up to visit him this morning, but I didn't get time to, and Mrs Ponsonby's coming around in half an hour. There's something she wants me to put to the committee.' Gran was chairwoman of the Welford Women's Institute.

'Hmmph!' Grandad gave Mandy a sideways look. 'That's most of the evening taken up then. That woman never uses one word when ten would do!'

Mandy chuckled. 'We could go and visit Wilfred. Couldn't we, James?'

He nodded.

'Would you, love?' Gran said. 'Bless you. It would put my mind at rest.'

If only *my* mind was at rest, Mandy thought. She wanted to make sure Wilfred was OK, but she also wanted to ask him about Matty. This time, she was determined to find out where the little old mare had gone. It was only days since the horse auction, but it felt like weeks since she had last set eyes on Matty.

'Why don't you pick some salad greens, Dorothy?' Grandad said to his wife. 'Mandy and James can take some to Wilfred.'

'Good idea,' Gran said. 'Those lettuces need picking before they bolt.'

Mandy knew that 'bolt' meant run to seed, but she grinned to herself, imagining the lettuces uprooting themselves and dashing off up the garden.

'Right, I'll leave you to it,' Grandad said. 'I'm just going to put a coat of wood preservative on this panel.' He winked at Mandy. 'Unless I'm needed.'

Gran gave him a playful push. 'Go on with you! I think we can manage.'

Mandy, James, and Gran picked their way past twiggy rows of young peas and beans. They pulled up lettuces, dug up young carrots and baby beetroot, and gathered bunches of spring onions.

'Here. You can pile them in this old basket,' Gran said, shaking loose soil from the roots. 'There. Don't they look a treat?'

Mandy nodded. Framed with ferny carrot tops and red-veined beet leaves, the vegetables looked as colourful as a Harvest Festival display. 'Wilfred's going to love these.'

A few minutes later there was a knock on the front door. Gran went to open it. With a sinking heart, Mandy heard her say, 'Oh, hello, Amelia. You're early.'

'I prefer to be prompt,' said a rich, bossy voice. 'Punctuality is my middle name.'

'I thought it was Bossy!' joked James.

Mrs Ponsonby sailed into the cottage, resplendent in a powder blue dress and a matching flowery hat. Pandora was, as usual, under her arm, a matching ribbon holding the fur out of her eyes. Toby, her mongrel dog, was trotting by her side.

'Uh-oh.' *Time to make an exit*, thought Mandy. She signalled to James and he nodded eagerly. Stooping to give Toby a hasty pat, they made their way out of the front door, saying their goodbyes as they went.

'Tut, tut! Young people today. Always in a hurry...' Mrs Ponsonby's fussy voice faded as Mandy paused on the drive to loop the basket over her handlebars.

They pedalled through the village and on towards Wilfred's cottage. On the outskirts, they crested the final hill and the cottage came into view.

'This is getting to be a habit!' James said with a grin, propping his bike against the new fence.

'Maybe we should bring our tents next time!' Mandy replied.

Wilfred's cottage had that same deserted look to it. She rapped the horse-shaped knocker. There was a movement of the kitchen curtains, then a hurried scuffling sound from inside the cottage.

'What can he be doing in there?' said James.

'I don't know,' Mandy answered.

After a long pause, they heard the sound of bolts being drawn. Wilfred opened the door a crack, giving them only a glimpse of the shadowy interior.

'Now then,' he said, his usual friendly greeting, but his voice sounded thin and wary. His flyaway white hair looked as if it hadn't been combed in days.

'Hi, Wilfred,' Mandy said with a warm smile. 'We've brought you some vegetables from Gran's garden.'

She thought the old man looked very tired and drawn, but he returned her smile. 'That's very kind of you, lass.' He reached for the basket. 'Tell your gran thanks. Much appreciated.'

Mandy kept a hold on the basket. 'We haven't seen you in the village lately,' she said.

'No. I've not been about much,' Wilfred said vaguely. 'I keep myself to myself. It's best that way.'

'I'd love to go and visit Matty . . .' Mandy began, trying a new tack. 'If you would just tell me where . . .'

'Er . . . I have to go now, lass,' Wilfred said, looking flustered.

He began to close the door, but got the basket caught in the doorway. As he opened the door to free it, the frayed cuff of his cardigan snagged on a loose piece of wicker.

'Oh, blast!' Wilfred muttered in dismay, as the basket tipped forward. The front door swung open. Spring onions flew everywhere, carrots bounced off the step, baby beetroots rolled into the house.

'Oh!' James hurried forward, bending to gather up an escaping lettuce.

While Wilfred was still trying to untangle himself from the basket, Mandy stepped inside the doorway to chase carrots and beetroots down the hall.

'Oh, dear me,' Wilfred said in a panicky voice, following as Mandy and James advanced into the cottage, their hands full. 'It's all right. I can manage now. Really, there's no need for you to come in . . .'

But Mandy was already inside the big old-fashioned kitchen. She plonked the vegetables in the deep sink, her mind registering that things looked very cluttered and untidy.

'Sorry about all the mess.' Wilfred shifted uneasily, looking embarrassed. 'I spend all my time in here now,' he said, a fleeting sadness passing over his face. 'I don't need much space. And I feel closest to Rose in here.'

Mandy nodded, feeling sad and a little puzzled. It wasn't like the Wilfred she knew to live in such chaos. But as she looked around Mandy realised that it wasn't just ordinary living mess that cluttered the kitchen. The oak dresser was piled with

ornaments that had come from the sitting room at
the back of the cottage. She remembered dusting
those vases in the sitting room when she had come
to the cottage with Gran, to help out when Rose
had been ill.

On one shelf there was Rose's collection of china
horses, and the little foal Mandy had bought for
Rose's last birthday.

There too was the special photo, the one of Rose
standing with a much younger Matty. Sunlight
picked out the silver in the mare's coat. Rose's hair
was dark and her face was creased in a bright smile.
A hand-written inscription in the corner read, 'My
Matty'.

It seemed as though Wilfred had moved these
things from the sitting room out of harm's way. *But
why?* Mandy wondered. It was very curious.

'Well – thanks again,' Wilfred said, looking more
agitated and worried. 'It was lovely to see you . . .'
He began trying to usher them to the door, the
sleeves of his tattered old cardigan trailing over his
thin hands.

Then Mandy noticed the rolled-up rug leaning in
one corner. It was the one that usually covered the
sitting room floor. Whatever was going on?

'Wilfred—' she began. Then she broke off in
amazement, as a most unexpected – but familiar –

sound rang out. The sound of a horse neighing.

But not just any horse . . .

James looked at her, his mouth hanging open.

For a moment, Mandy was too stunned to utter a word. Could it really be . . . 'Matty?' she gasped.

Wilfred's shoulders sagged. He looked up at her and gave a deep sigh. 'Yes, lass,' he said gently. 'You've found me out.'

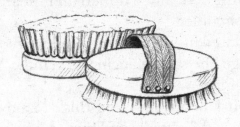

Seven

'You'd best come through,' Wilfred said, leading the way.

Mandy's heart was beating fast as she and James followed him. She couldn't believe it. Wilfred had been keeping Matty in the house!

The curtains were drawn in the sitting room and in the semi-darkness Matty's pale coat glowed. Something clicked in the back of Mandy's mind, but she was too delighted to see Matty again to pay attention to it. The elderly little horse turned her head and whickered softly in greeting.

'Oh, Matty.' Mandy rushed forward and threw her arms around the mare's neck. 'It's so lovely to see you!'

She looked up at Wilfred, her eyes shining as

Matty whinnied and rubbed her head against Mandy's shoulder.

James stared in amazement. 'You knew something was strange,' he said, glancing at Mandy. 'You were right all along!'

'Yes, but I never expected this!' Mandy hugged Matty's neck delightedly and buried her face in the pale mane.

Wilfred looked at Matty, his lined old face wistful. 'When it came to the morning of the horse sale, I just couldn't bear to part with her. Not with her being Rose's favourite, and all. But I just didn't know what to do. I had nowhere to put her.'

Thinking of the photo of Rose with Matty, Mandy felt a lump rise in her throat. She swallowed hard and looked around. Wilfred shouldn't be keeping Matty in here, but he had done his best. The furniture had been pushed against the wall and covered with sheets. Straw had been spread on the stone floor. A bucket of water stood in the corner and a hay-net hung from a hook on the door.

Mandy stroked Matty's velvety nose, noticing that the little mare's eyes were bright and her coat soft and glossy. She certainly seemed happy enough, but for how much longer?

'You're not planning to go on keeping her in the house, are you?' she asked Wilfred worriedly.

Wilfred ran his fingers through his straggly white hair. 'No, lass. It was only supposed to be for a couple of days. Just until I worked something out. I've made countless phone calls, trying to find someone I know and trust who'll take Matty. But it's been a week now, and I've almost run out of people to try.'

He sank down wearily on to the arm of a sofa. 'To tell you the truth,' he said, shoulders drooping, 'I've been at my wits' end with all this. I don't know if I'm coming or going.'

Mandy remembered the cluttered kitchen. Poor Wilfred. She thought Matty looked in better shape than he did. It all seemed too much for the old man.

'It must have been hard to keep this a secret,' said James.

'Aye, lad, it was that.' Wilfred looked up. 'I was worried at first that someone would hear Matty, but all that racket going on next door hid any noise she made. It's been harder to keep things secret since the campsite opened. But Matty doesn't need much exercise. She's been content with going out at night, when there's no one about. But I know this can't go on much longer – it's not fair on either of us.'

Mandy and James shook their heads sympathetically.

Then Mandy gasped. 'Oh!' She looked at James. Suddenly everything fell into place. The silver-grey horse and her rider – a man with white hair.

'The ghostly horseman!' said James, guessing her thoughts.

Wilfred looked puzzled. 'What's that?'

'Some of the campers have seen you on Matty at night,' Mandy explained. 'But they knew there were no horses stabled near here any more.'

James took up the story, 'So, they thought it was a ghostly horse and rider! In the mist and moonlight you must have looked quite spooky. People are saying the campsite's haunted! Sam Western's furious about the whole thing.'

Wilfred shook his head from side to side. 'By heck! I had no idea that all this was going on. I seem to have caused a lot of trouble.'

'You didn't mean to,' Mandy said.

'No, I didn't,' agreed Wilfred. 'But Sam Western won't see it like that. Once he hears about this there'll be fireworks.'

'Huh! He won't hear anything from me,' muttered James.

'Nor me,' Mandy found herself echoing. It might not be right to keep Matty in the house, but she knew that Wilfred's intentions had been well-meaning.

'You mean – you'll keep my secret?' Wilfred looked surprised, but pleased.

'Yes. But on one condition,' Mandy said. She saw James looking at her curiously.

'What's that?' Wilfred said.

'That until Matty goes to her new home, James and I can help you look after her!' James smiled and nodded in agreement.

'We-ell.' Wilfred considered their offer, then his face broadened in a smile. 'All right. I must admit, I'd be glad of an extra hand.'

'Great!' said James, with a perfectly straight face. 'Then you'll be even more pleased to have four!'

They all laughed.

'I don't like the idea of you two fibbing for me, mind,' Wilfred said.

'It's not exactly fibbing,' Mandy said. 'Not if we just don't talk about you and Matty to anyone in the village.'

'That's right,' agreed James.

'And Mum and Dad won't tell anyone,' Mandy began eagerly, 'once we explain. They might be able to help . . .' She paused, noticing that Wilfred was looking a bit sheepish.

'I'd rather you didn't tell your parents either. Not just yet, lass,' he said. 'I've got one last person to see about Matty. I'd really like to find her a home myself. I've got my pride, see? I know I got into a mess with the business and everything, but if I can just see Matty settled, well – it'll make things right. I owe that to Rose.'

'But what if this person can't take Matty either?' Mandy asked worriedly.

Wilfred lifted his head, a determined look on his face. 'Matty's wellbeing has to come first,' he said stoutly. 'If this last lead comes to nothing in the next few days, I'll be only too glad to ask for Adam's help.'

Mandy nodded. 'OK.' She knew her soft-hearted dad would understand if she kept Wilfred's secret. It was in a good cause. Mum might be another matter. But she'd worry about that when it came to it.

James nodded in agreement.

'Ah, well,' Wilfred said with a grin. 'And with any luck, it'll only be for another day or two. Once Matty's settled in to her new home, I couldn't care less if the whole story comes out and that puffed-up Sam Western complains until he's blue in the face!'

Mandy chuckled. Wilfred was beginning to sound more like his jaunty old self. She put out a hand and rubbed Matty's nose. 'Can James and I start helping you with Matty now?'

She was itching to make a fuss of the little horse.

It seemed so long since she had groomed that beautiful silver-grey coat and braided the flowing mane and tail.

'I don't see why not,' Wilfred said, smiling. He reached up and twitched the curtains open a little way, so that a shaft of sunlight, swirling with dust motes, poured into the room. By the extra light, Mandy saw again how tired and gaunt the old man looked. James had noticed too.

'I think we can manage in here by ourselves,' Mandy said, casually.

'Easy as pie!' James said, following her lead.

Wilfred drew himself up. He seemed about to protest, then he changed his mind. 'To tell you the truth I'm dying for a cup of tea,' he said. 'Go on with you then. I'll just show you where everything is.'

'Right,' said Mandy, pushing up her sleeves.

Wilfred took them out to the tiny back yard. There was an old coal bunker beside the back door. Wilfred opened it. Inside, there was a plastic bin with oats and bran and two small piles of hay and straw.

'Got everything you need? Then I'll leave you to it.' Wilfred went back into the kitchen.

'Oh, look,' Mandy said. 'He's kept all Matty's grooming equipment.' She took out the plastic tray with all its different brushes, curry combs, and sponges. There was even a straw wisp for massaging, that Wilfred had made himself. Everything was well-used but spotlessly clean.

'He really does love that horse,' James said.

Mandy sighed. 'If only there was some way he could keep her.' *But where*? she thought. *You can't keep a horse for long without stables and land.*

Back in the sitting room, Mandy and James set to. It was hard work. First Mandy raked out the old straw and heaped it into the tiny yard. There was no room for a muck heap, so James forked it into the black bin bags Wilfred had given them.

'No wonder Wilfred looks so tired,' said James.

Mandy nodded, imagining Wilfred having to stay up late every night to exercise Matty.

Mandy swept the stone floor while James fetched fresh bedding. 'There's not much straw left in the bunker,' he said as he helped Mandy spread the new straw evenly with a rake. 'We'll have to remember to tell Wilfred.'

While James swilled out and re-filled the water bucket, Mandy saw to the hay-net. As soon as she'd hung it back on its hook, Matty stretched her neck and began pulling out wisps of fresh hay with her angled yellow teeth.

'It's so lovely to see her again, isn't it?' Mandy

said, running a hand down the mare's sleek, dappled flank. Matty's ears swivelled as if she knew what Mandy was saying. 'I wish I'd got a treat for her.'

'You should have brought some of your dad's carrot sticks!' joked James.

Mandy laughed. 'I know just what Dad would say: "She's welcome to them"!'

'Hang on a sec. Why don't we give her a couple of those carrots your gran sent for Wilfred?'

'Good idea,' Mandy said. 'I'm sure Wilfred won't mind.'

They found him in the kitchen. Wilfred had been busy too. Clean crockery was piled on the draining board and freshly-scrubbed pots and pans hung from their hooks.

'Now then,' he said, looking more relaxed than they had seen him for weeks. 'How are you two getting on?'

'We've finished the mucking out,' Mandy said.

'Already? My, you're hard workers!'

'Oh, we don't hang about!' James said with a grin.

'Can we have a couple of Gran's carrots for Matty?' asked Mandy.

'You go right ahead,' Wilfred said.

Mandy rinsed off the soil, then chopped the carrots into lengthways strips; she knew that square or round pieces could get stuck in a horse's throat.

Wilfred came through and watched as she fed the sweet young carrots to Matty.

He looked down at the clean fresh straw. 'You've done a grand job,' he said.

Mandy smiled. That made all their hard work worthwhile. The little horse finished crunching up the carrots. Whickering softly, she nudged against Mandy's jeans pocket.

'I'm sorry I haven't brought you a red apple,' Mandy said with a happy grin. 'But I'll bring you one next time. That's a promise!'

She gave Matty a final pat. She hated leaving the little mare so soon after finding her again, but it wouldn't be for long.

Wilfred came to the front door to wave them goodbye. 'Thanks a lot, you two.'

'That's OK, Wilfred.'

The old man coughed. 'Matty really appreciated the visit, you know,' he said, his voice sounding gruff. 'We two old 'uns rub along happily together, but Matty misses Rose. She's used to a woman's company.'

'We'll come again before school tomorrow...' Mandy began. 'Oh, I almost forgot. You'll need some more straw soon.'

'Oh, dear me,' Wilfred murmured, beginning to look worried again. 'I knew I was getting low. It's going to arouse suspicion in the village if I'm seen buying straw.'

'Don't worry. You leave that to us,' Mandy said firmly.

She had no idea how she and James were going to get some straw for Matty, but she was sure they would think of something.

Eight

Mandy soon found out that it was more difficult to keep Wilfred's secret than she'd imagined.

'Your gran said you took some fresh veg up to Wilfred the other evening,' Mrs Hope said.

Mandy had changed out of her school uniform. She and her mum were eating tea alone before early evening surgery started. Her dad was still out doing routine inoculations at some of the isolated farms.

'Mmm,' Mandy said, taking a huge bite of crusty french bread. She chewed slowly, hoping her mum wouldn't ask any more questions.

'Did you see Wilfred?' Mrs Hope prompted.

Mandy nodded, making 'uh-huh' sounds.

'And how was he?'

Mandy tried to look casual. 'Fine,' she mimed with her mouth still full.

Mrs Hope stood up and put a white lab coat on over her clothes. She frowned, looking closely at her daughter with suspicious green eyes, but she only said, 'Well, I'm glad to hear he's OK.'

'Phew!' Mandy sighed. It had sounded so simple when she had promised Wilfred that she wouldn't talk about him or Matty!

She and James had been going up to help Wilfred with Matty after school for the past couple of days. Not only was it becoming more difficult to keep Wilfred's secret, the quest for straw had become urgent.

Mandy bumped into Simon as she was slipping inside the Animal Ark store room. Inside there were tins and packets of every kind of animal food and enough straw to bed down an elephant. She had been hoping that she could smuggle out some straw for Matty.

'Hi, there,' said Simon. 'What are you after?' His short blond hair stuck up in spikes, where he had dragged his fingers through it.

'Um . . . some straw,' Mandy blurted out guiltily.

'Need some for Flopsy, Mopsy, and Cottontail, do you?' Simon said helpfully.

Mandy's three pet rabbits were in their run, their

hutch cleaned out and pristine, but she nodded, watching as he grabbed handfuls of straw and stuffed it into a plastic carrier bag.

'There you are. I'll put it outside the back door for you.' Simon's eyes were friendly behind his glasses.

'Thanks,' Mandy said. There was only enough straw there to cover about half a metre of Wilfred's stone floor, but it was a start.

'Are you in a mad rush?' asked Simon. 'Your mum's got someone coming into the treatment room with a pet you might like to see.'

Mandy followed him eagerly. She could always find time to see a new patient.

'Oh.' Mandy's eyes widened when she saw the tortoise. Its shell was a shiny dome as big as a beach ball. The head and legs were drawn in closely beneath the shell.

'He's handsome, isn't he?' said the owner. Mrs Bland was a smartly dressed woman who owned a haulage business in Walton. 'I've had Thomas almost thirty years.'

'He's lovely,' Mandy agreed. 'What's wrong with him, Mum?'

'He's been losing weight,' Emily Hope said, turning to Mrs Bland. 'What do you feed him on?'

'All kinds of things, lettuce, dandelion leaves. He

loves strawberries, but he hasn't even been eating them lately.' She looked worried. 'Is it something serious?'

Mrs Hope asked Simon to help while she examined the heavy tortoise. Simon held Thomas's shell, careful to avoid the scaly feet that scrabbled against the examination table. Thomas's claws were strong and curved and capable of inflicting a nasty gash.

'See if you can coax him to put his head out, love,' Mrs Hope said to Mandy.

Mandy spoke to the tortoise gently and stroked one of his forelegs reassuringly. After a few moments, Thomas stuck out his long wrinkled neck. He blinked slowly, then yawned.

'Ah, I see the problem,' her mum said at once. 'Can you see it, Mandy?'

'His beak looks a bit strange,' Mandy said.

'That's right. It's overgrown.' Mrs Hope turned to Thomas's owner. 'That's why he's having a problem eating. I'll just trim his beak and he'll be fine.'

'Oh, dear,' Mrs Bland said. 'It won't hurt him, will it?'

'No,' said Mrs Hope. She selected a pair of stainless steel clippers from the sterilising unit. 'It's just like cutting your finger nails.'

Mandy helped Simon hold Thomas still. A couple of snips, carefully angled so that Thomas's beak kept the same shape, and it was done.

'Oh, that's a relief!' Mrs Bland said. 'Thank you so much.' She picked Thomas up and went out of the treatment room.

'Thanks for your help, Mandy,' Simon said. 'Are you off now? Don't forget that bag of—'

'Er, right,' Mandy said quickly, catching her mum's eye. 'Got to dash! Bye, Simon. Bye, Mum! I'll be back in a couple of hours.'

She hurried out into the reception area before her mum could ask any awkward questions. Jean Knox was behind the desk, her head bent over the appointments book as she rifled through its pages.

'Oh, hello, Mandy,' Jean looked up and gave a flustered smile. 'Did you want your mum? She's in the treatment room.'

'Hi, Jean! It's all right. I've just seen her.'

'Righto, dear,' Jean said, still searching for something. 'Now where have I put those . . .'

'They're on the chain around your neck,' Mandy said, trying not to giggle. Jean was always losing her spectacles!

'Thanks, dear!' Jean called out as Mandy headed for the door into the cottage. 'Silly me. It's a good thing my head's not loose!'

Mandy took three red apples from the bowl of fruit on the kitchen table. Pausing only to fetch the plastic bag of straw, she hurried out into the lane.

James was waiting at the village green, his bike leaning against the neatly clipped hedge. He looked bored. He had a piece of grass held between his thumbs and was blowing on it to make a trumpeting sound.

'Sorry I'm late.' As Mandy lifted the carrier bag off her handlebars, James peered at it, a dubious expression on his face. 'I know!' she said with a rueful smile. 'It wouldn't even last a hamster five minutes!'

'You said it!' James grinned. 'Couldn't you get any more?'

Mandy shook her head, 'No. Simon would have been suspicious.'

'Simon?' James said. 'What's he got to do with it?'

He got no answer. Mandy had suddenly had a brainwave. 'I know where there's *loads* of straw!' she said, turning her bike around. 'Come on.'

'Where to?' asked James.

'Grandad's shed! He and Gran are away on one of their trips today, but he keeps the key under a stone in the rockery.'

A few minutes later, they had arrived at Lilac

Cottage. They stood looking at the bale of straw that Grandad planned to strew over his strawberry beds.

'Perfect!' Mandy exclaimed.

'Oh,no! We can't,' James said, his face a picture of concern.

'It's the only way,' Mandy said decisively. 'Matty needs bedding. Where else are we going to get this much straw?'

'But won't your grandad notice it's been stolen?'

'Borrowed,' Mandy said firmly. 'He said he wasn't planning to use it for a day or two. We'll have thought of a way to replace it by then.'

'Will we?' James took a deep breath. 'OK. What if we do "borrow" it? How are we going to get it up to Wilfred?'

Mandy bit her lip in concentration. 'It's not that heavy. I know! We'll prop it on our bikes and wheel it up there.'

'We could do,' James said, still looking doubtful. 'But someone in the village is bound to see us. You can't exactly disguise a whopping great bale of straw!'

Mandy grinned. If you were determined enough there was always a way. 'You can if you cover it with something.'

'Like what?'

'This!' She reached up and took down an old rug that Grandad put over his cold frame in frosty weather.

James eyed the rug's yellow zig-zag pattern. 'It's a bit bright.'

'It's all we have. It'll just have to do.'

'OK,' said James. 'Let's do it. I'll fetch the bikes.'

After a bit of a struggle, they managed to get the bale positioned so that it was balanced between the bikes. Mandy covered it with the rug, tying it down with some of Grandad's garden twine. She took a grip on her handlebars, while James grabbed hold of his on the opposite side. 'Ready? Off we go.'

At first it was a bit of a joke. James made her laugh, thinking of the silly things they could say if anyone asked them what they were doing. 'How about – we're having an evening picnic and we're very, very hungry!' he suggested. Then they reached the first hill and they had no breath for talking, let alone laughing.

Almost an hour later, tired, red-faced and dying for a cold drink, they trundled up to Wilfred's front door. This time, the old man was expecting them. He opened the door almost at once.

'By gum! What's that contraption you've got there?' he said, his white eyebrows shooting up in amazement.

'It's . . . straw under here,' Mandy could only gasp.

'For . . . Matty,' James managed to get out.

'Best bring it round the back sharpish then,' Wilfred said, catching on fast. 'Did anybody see you bringing it up here?'

'No,' Mandy explained, once she'd got her breath back. 'It was amazing. We didn't meet a single person.' There had been a sticky moment, when they had to go past the front of the post office. But Mrs McFarlane had not noticed them.

'It's champion. Just what I need,' Wilfred said. He helped lift the bale off the bikes and stowed it in the old coal bunker, then he took his purse out of his trouser pocket. 'How much do I owe you?'

'We-ell,' Mandy began, looking a bit sheepish. 'It's a bit hard to say.'

'Eh? How's that, lass?'

'It's not exactly ours. We've borrowed it from my grandad's shed.'

'Dear oh dear!' Wilfred began to chuckle. 'Have you now? And you wheeled it all through the village! Tom Hope will skin me alive if he thinks I put you up to this!'

'No, he won't. We'll explain,' Mandy said. 'Besides, he might not notice it's gone.'

'And pigs might fly,' muttered James. He had a sudden thought. 'What did you do with that plastic bag of straw that Simon gave you?'

'Uh-oh.' Mandy's hand flew to her mouth. 'I left it in Grandad's shed!'

'Oh, dear oh dear!' Wilfred was laughing so much that his shoulders were shaking. 'I'd like to be a fly on the wall when Tom finds out that his bale of straw has magically turned into a few handfuls in a plastic bag!'

Mandy and James began laughing too. It was hard not to see the funny side and Wilfred's laugh was infectious.

Wilfred wiped his eyes on the back of his hand. 'My, you young 'uns are enterprising, I'll give you that! Come inside and have a cold drink.'

Mandy and James collapsed on kitchen chairs while Wilfred rummaged in cupboards. 'Oh, dear. I've only got orange squash, I'm afraid. Nothing fancy like lemonade or coke.'

'Squash is fine, thanks,' Mandy said. She drained her glass in one go, then jumped up and put her used glass in the sink. 'Can we go and see Matty now?'

'I thought you'd never ask,' Wilfred said. 'Go on through.'

As they entered, Matty turned her head and whinnied softly.

'Hello, old girl,' Mandy said, putting her arms

round Matty's neck. She laid her cheek against the mare's satiny shoulder.

Matty blew softly on Mandy's cheek. Then she dipped her neck and nudged at Mandy's arm.

'Yes, I remembered your apples!' Mandy laughed. 'Red ones. Your favourite.'

Matty's soft lips nuzzled her palm as she took the first apple. Mandy stroked Matty's dark grey nose as the mare crunched up the fruit and chewed contentedly. Mandy was longing to slip a headcollar on to her and lead her out into the fresh air.

Just then Wilfred came into the back room. 'I've just been on the phone to that friend I told you about,' he said to Mandy and James. 'The one who I thought might have Matty.'

'Is he going to take her?' Mandy asked eagerly.

Wilfred stroked his chin, looking weary. 'He says he's not sure. He thinks she's a bit too old.' He shook his head, looking desperate. 'I was banking on him taking her. I don't know who else to ask.'

'What about the horse auctions?' suggested James in his practical way. 'Couldn't you sell Matty there? Like you sold your other horses?'

Wilfred looked at him and shook his head slowly. 'I can't face her going to strangers, lad – not if there's the slightest chance of an alternative. I've been trying to think if there's someone I haven't tried. There *must* be somebody I know who'd want her.'

But time was running out. Mandy felt it and she knew Wilfred did too. He had to find a solution, and very soon, for Matty's sake.

Wilfred stroked Matty's neck. 'She needs a field where she can run free,' he said sadly. 'I'm trying my best, but I'm afraid it'll have to be moonlight jaunts for just a bit longer.'

'We can come up and help you exercise her, can't we, James?' Mandy said.

James nodded.

The old man brightened. 'You'd be doing me a favour. But are you sure you'll be allowed up here so late at night?'

'Oh, yes,' Mandy said. 'Well, for the next couple of days, anyway. It's Friday tomorrow, so we get to stay up later – no school the following day.'

James grinned. 'I can feel another badger watch coming on!'

The next day, Mandy could hardly concentrate on her lessons. Rather than go straight over to help Wilfred after school, she and James planned to go over later, in order to be around for Matty's exercise time.

As soon as she had helped clear up after tea,

Mandy excused herself. On the way to her room she picked out three apples from the fruit bowl.

A short while later, she popped her head around the sitting room door and waved to her dad. Mr Hope was sprawled in front of the TV, tired out after a long day. He waved back, a half-eaten apple in his hand.

'Got everything for the badger watch, love?' her mum asked.

'Yep.' Mandy patted her hold-all. 'Torch and binoculars,' she said. *Riding hat. And three more apples for Matty*, she added to herself.

'OK then. Have a good time but take care. See you just after ten – no later!' Mrs Hope went into the sitting room.

Mandy flew down the hall and almost tripped over a loose shoelace. She paused in the open front doorway to tie it and heard her dad say, 'Was that Mandy I just saw flitting through! Or was it a mirage?'

'I wish I had half her energy,' Mrs Hope said with a chuckle. There was a pause, then she said, 'I think I'll have an apple as well.'

'Oh sorry. This was the last one left,' her dad said. 'Funny that. The fruit bowl was almost full this morning . . .'

Mandy was up like a flash and out of the front door before her dad had finished the sentence.

*   *   *

'Oh, heck,' said James when she told him about the apples. 'You don't think your mum and dad have caught on to us do you?'

'Not yet,' Mandy said. 'But if Grandad phones about his straw they're bound to put two and two together.'

'And work out exactly what's been going on these past few days,' groaned James.

They reached Wilfred's cottage and stopped outside on the road. Just a few metres away was the sign that read, 'Western's Campsite'. And past that, the gate stood wide open.

Mandy remembered the scene in the campsite from the night of Sparky's accident. The few lights glowing in the darkness had seemed only to emphasise the field's emptiness. She imagined Flora's low tent, all lit up from inside, looking cosy and welcoming.

'I bet Sparky's being spoilt rotten,' James said. 'Tea in bed and everything!'

Mandy grinned. 'Flora brought him into Animal Ark for his check-up yesterday evening. Dad says his leg's healing really well.'

'Good,' James said. 'It's Saturday tomorrow, so we'll have time to go and visit him.' He followed Mandy round to the back of Wilfred's cottage. 'At least we needn't worry about him chasing after ghostly horses tonight.'

'No,' Mandy agreed. 'Flora's determined that he rests that leg. She's probably got his lead looped to the tent post!'

Wilfred was waiting for them with Matty in the back sitting room. While they changed Matty's straw and water, Wilfred put her in a bridle. 'It's safer for leading her near the road,' he said.

He brought the reins over Matty's head and offered them to Mandy. 'Do you want to take her? James and I will follow you.'

'Oh yes,' Mandy breathed. She quickly put on her riding hat, then took the reins. She was a bit nervous as she led Matty out of the back door.

The tiny yard was cramped, so it was difficult to turn the little horse and bring her down the side of the cottage, but Matty behaved beautifully, bending her neck so that Mandy didn't need to pull her round. 'Good girl,' Mandy said, patting her neck.

'That was neatly done, Mandy,' Wilfred said.

Mandy smiled. 'Rose showed me how to do that.'

They trooped down the side of the new fence to a narrow strip of field at the roadside. Wilfred explained that they must warm Matty up slowly. 'As she spends the day just standing in the house, there's the risk of a strained muscle if she's ridden too much without a careful warming-up.'

Mandy and James took it in turn to ride Matty, walking and trotting the elderly mare while Wilfred supervised. Mandy sat firmly in the saddle, enjoying every moment. It was wonderful to be riding the little mare again.

'Once you've had your rides, I'll take Matty out on the lanes,' Wilfred said. 'She enjoys a good long hack.'

Matty seemed to be enjoying the exercise. She moved easily and fluidly, the muscles working under her pale coat. Mandy was watching as James trotted by on Matty, when she noticed a slight reluctance in the horse's movements. Matty seemed to be hanging back, and pulling a little on the reins.

Mandy pointed it out to Wilfred. 'I think Matty's had enough exercise for now,' she said.

Wilfred frowned. 'We've not been out here all that long.' He ran his hands down Matty's flanks and checked her legs. 'She's not getting lame,' he said. 'But I think we'll take her back inside.'

Back in the house, Wilfred hung up the tackle, then began wiping Matty down with a handful of straw. Mandy helped dry off the mare's coat, then give her a brisk brush down. The mare's head was dropping a little and she was shifting her weight from foot to foot. Now and then she pawed the ground.

'I think I'll make her up a warm bran mash,' Wilfred said thoughtfully. He turned to Mandy and James. 'It's late. I think you two'd best be getting home.'

'OK,' Mandy said. 'We'll come back again in the morning.'

'We can stay longer tomorrow,' James put in, 'as it's Saturday.'

'Right you are,' Wilfred said. 'And thanks again. You've been a great help.'

Mandy and James gave Matty a final pat. 'See you tomorrow.'

At the door, Mandy glanced back at Matty. The mare raised her head and whickered softly.

Mandy was quiet as she and James cycled home. 'What's wrong?' asked James, as they drew to a halt outside his house.

'It's Matty. I think something's wrong with her.'

'She seemed all right when we left,' said James.

'I know, but I've got a funny feeling.'

'Uh-oh.' James looked at her. 'What are you going to do?'

Mandy shrugged, miserably. 'I don't know. I wish I could talk to Mum or Dad.'

'You can't!' James replied. 'We promised Wilfred.'

'I know,' Mandy said. 'But if Matty's sick I've got to do something! Wilfred needs help.'

The problem occupied her thoughts as she cycled the short distance to Animal Ark. It was still on her mind as she got ready for bed. She lay awake for ages, staring into the dark and worrying about Wilfred and Matty.

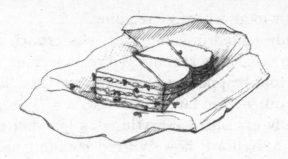

Nine

Early next morning, Mandy jumped out of bed and threw on some jeans and a jumper. She had to know if Matty was all right. She dashed downstairs, all set to excuse herself from breakfast and her morning chores in Animal Ark. Her dad was on the telephone in the hall and the look on his face stopped her in her tracks.

'Sounds like it could be colic,' he said. 'What's she doing now? Right. OK. I'll get over there straight away.'

Mandy's heart plummeted. 'That was Wilfred, wasn't it? Oh, I knew Matty didn't look well! Can I come with you?'

Mr Hope looked at his daughter's flushed face. 'I think you'd better. Wait here a minute. I'll just tell your mum where we're going.'

Mandy waited impatiently. It was crunch time, time to own up to keeping Wilfred's secret.

Mr Hope reappeared a few moments later. 'Right. Come on. We can talk on the way.'

Mandy explained everything as her dad drove through Welford; how Wilfred couldn't bear to part with Matty, but knew he couldn't keep her in the house much longer. And how she and James had been helping him over the past few days. 'He really wanted to find a new home for her himself, Dad. To make up for getting into such a mess with his business. He says he owes it to Rose.'

Mr Hope listened intently. 'So,' he said when she'd finished, 'you were right about Matty all along.' He gave her a sideways look. 'All this explains a few things.'

'Like – a bowlful of missing apples?' Mandy said, putting her chin on her chest and sliding down into her seat.

'And having hardly seen you after school for days on end. And an Animal Ark carrier bag of straw in place of a full bale, in your grandad's shed!'

Mandy slid down further. 'Oh, you know about that too?'

'Uh-huh, but never mind that now,' her dad said.

'Tell me how Matty was the last time you saw her.'

Mandy smiled. Her dad never made a fuss about little things, when there was something important at stake. She explained how Matty had kept shifting her weight about and pawing at the ground.

'Was she looking at her sides and fretting? Trying to bite at herself?'

Mandy shook her head. 'No. She seemed fine when we left.'

She wished she could tell him more, but Wilfred would be able to supply other details. As soon as Mr Hope parked the Land-rover, Wilfred rushed out of his cottage to greet them.

'She's took badly, Adam. I don't know what to do for her.'

Mr Hope clapped Wilfred on the arm. 'Lead the way,' he said, in his calm straightforward way.

Mandy followed them into the back room. Matty's head hung down and her ears were laid back. She could see at once that the elderly mare's belly looked quite tight and swollen. Matty turned her head when she saw Mandy and whickered softly, her dark eyes glazed with pain.

'Oh you poor thing.' Concern strangled Mandy's voice. She reached up and stroked Matty's cheek soothingly, feeling relieved that her dad was here.

'Has she eaten or drunk anything recently?' Mr Hope asked Wilfred.

Wilfred shook his head. 'No, lad. Not since yesterday when I gave her some bran mash. I found her like this, this morning.'

Matty snorted restlessly, lifting each of her back feet in turn.

'Right.' Mr Hope stripped off his jacket and went into action. 'Mandy would you help me, please?'

Mandy forced herself to be practical. It helped distract her a bit. As she opened her dad's bag and passed him his stethoscope she found herself growing calmer. She watched Mr Hope examine Matty with gentle, skilful hands and then listen to her stomach.

'Hmmm.' Her dad stroked his dark beard thoughtfully. 'I'm going to give her a painkiller,' he told Wilfred. 'That'll make her more comfortable. And I'm going to need blood and fluid samples from her stomach.'

'Is it serious?' Wilfred asked. He put a steadying hand on Matty's neck, as Mr Hope took the samples. 'There now, old girl.'

Mr Hope was screwing on tops and labelling plastic tubes. 'It's not looking good, I'm afraid,' he said gently.

'Do you know what's causing the colic, Dad?'

Mandy asked worriedly. She knew colic simply meant abdominal pain and that there were many reasons for it. The most serious kinds of colic could need an operation.

'We'll know more once I get the test results,' her dad answered. 'I'll have to go back to Animal Ark with these samples. Will you be all right here?'

Mandy smiled up at her dad. He hadn't even asked if she wanted to stay with Matty. He knew the answer already. 'I'll be fine.'

'Good girl.' Mr Hope patted her shoulder. 'I'll be back as soon as I can.'

The next couple of hours seemed like a lifetime. Matty did seem more comfortable after the pain-killer, but she was still restless. Mandy and Wilfred took turns to sit with her.

To pass the time they spoke about Rose and happier times at the stables. 'Rose really loved to see the children enjoying their rides,' Wilfred said with a smile. 'I promised Rose I'd take care of Matty. I don't know what I'll do if anything happens to her.'

'Don't worry. Dad'll help Matty,' Mandy said. 'He's a brilliant vet.'

'I know, lass,' Wilfred said. 'He always was a good

'un, was young Adam. Everyone knew Tom Hope's lad was a brainbox.'

It gave Mandy a warm feeling to think that her dad had lived in Welford all his life. He had been born in Lilac Cottage and the villagers thought of him as one of their own.

It was around noon when Mr Hope returned. Mandy heard him stride into the cottage and dump a package on the kitchen table. 'Egg and cress sandwiches,' he said. 'Enough for an army. I didn't think you'd have given much thought to food. How's Matty?'

'No better,' Wilfred said. 'Mandy's with her. Come on through.'

'What did the tests show, Dad?' Mandy asked impatiently.

'They weren't conclusive, I'm afraid,' Mr Hope replied, running an expert hand over Matty's rounded belly. 'We can rule out worms. I think we're looking at impaction or a twisted gut.'

Wilfred blanched. 'A twisted gut. That can be fatal, can't it?'

'Oh!' Mandy gasped. Matty couldn't be going to die!

'Hold on, Wilfred,' Mr Hope said calmly. 'I'm inclined to treat her for impaction.'

'Does that mean something is stuck in Matty's

bowel?' Mandy asked worriedly.

Her dad nodded. 'That's right. Material collects there and causes a blockage. We can try to clear it out with a drench.'

'But what if it *is* a twisted gut?' Wilfred said; his face seemed carved out of stone. 'Will my old girl have to have an operation?'

'Let's hope it won't come to that,' Mr Hope said, taking a length of tubing out of his bag. 'Have you got a clean bucket I can use?'

'Is an operation dangerous, Dad?' Mandy whispered, as she helped him mix the medication for the drench. She knew Mr Hope believed in always telling her the truth, even though it was hard to take sometimes.

'It would be very risky at Matty's age,' her dad said quietly, then in a normal voice, 'Right. The drench is ready. Can you steady Matty while I put in the tube, Wilfred?'

Matty made no protest, as Mr Hope put the tube in place, then fed her the medicine. Mandy patted her. 'Good girl.'

Mr Hope gently withdrew the stomach tube. 'OK. The next few hours are going to be crucial. She'll need watching at all times. If she doesn't shift the blockage soon, I may have to arrange for an emergency operation.'

'Can I stay here with you, Dad?' Mandy said at once. 'If Wilfred doesn't mind.'

Wilfred rubbed his unshaven cheeks. 'I don't know, lass. It could be a long job. Messy too.'

'I don't mind. I clean up messes at Animal Ark every day. Animals can't help it when they're sick.' She looked up at Wilfred, her blue eyes wide and pleading. 'And it would help Matty. You said yourself that she responds best to women.'

Mr Hope grinned. 'Persuasive, isn't she? She could be right about Matty though.'

Wilfred nodded. 'Aye, well. I'd be glad of any extra help. And your lass does have a way with Matty.'

Mr Hope winked at Mandy and ushered Wilfred through into the kitchen. 'Put that kettle on, Wilfred,' he said bracingly. 'We could have a wait on our hands.'

Mandy smiled to herself. Her dad had seen how tired the old man looked. It was his tactful way of getting Wilfred to relax and eat something.

'I'm going to have a chat with Wilfred in the kitchen,' Mr Hope said. 'Will you monitor Matty's pulse for me?'

Mandy nodded. 'And I'll call you if she starts rolling or sweating.'

Mandy heard Wilfred say, 'She knows her stuff.'

Mr Hope flashed Mandy one of his lopsided grins. 'She's had a good teacher!'

Half an hour passed and the low rumble of voices from the kitchen continued. Mandy knew that people found it easy to talk to her dad. After all his recent troubles, Wilfred probably needed to pour his heart out.

Mandy stroked Matty, speaking soothingly to her. 'Come on, girl. Get rid of all that nasty stuff that's blocking you up.'

The drench ought to work soon. It just had to, otherwise her dad would have to operate. She had a horrible feeling that Matty wouldn't survive that.

Mandy rested the tips of her fingers on the artery that passed over the edge of Matty's lower jaw, and counted the pulse beats. Fifty-five beats per minute. The pulse was fast, but not dangerously so.

Mandy kept checking the pulse at regular intervals. Now and then, the little mare shifted uncomfortably, her head nodding up and down. There was nothing to do but wait. Mandy tried not to give in to feelings of helplessness and fear. She spoke gently and encouragingly to Matty.

'Come on. You can do it,' she repeated over and over, as if will power alone would help shift the blockage.

After a while her eyelids started to droop. It was warm in Wilfred's sitting room and she hadn't slept well the previous night. Then Matty snorted and moved position. Mandy jumped, wide awake immediately. She rested her fingers on Matty's lower jaw, feeling for the mare's pulse. Eighty beats a minute.

'Oh, no!' She was out of the room in an instant and bursting into the kitchen. 'Dad! Come quickly. Matty's worse!'

Wilfred and Mr Hope hurtled into the back room, Mandy at their side. Matty had sunk to her knees. As Mandy watched, she rolled on to her side. Her breathing was shallow and her eyes rolled back in fear, as ripples threaded across her swollen belly.

Mandy threw herself down beside the mare. She cradled Matty's head in her lap as Mr Hope examined her.

She bit her lip. 'What's wrong with her, Dad?'

Mr Hope shook his head. 'It looks like the pain's getting worse and she seems to be panicking.'

'No,' Mandy murmured. She couldn't give up. Not now.

Her dad got up and reached for his bag. 'I'm going to give her a stronger painkiller, and a sedative to calm her down.'

'Oh, Matty,' Mandy whispered. 'You *must* get well. Wilfred needs you.'

Matty shuddered and raised her head, the whites of her eyes showing in pain and panic. Mr Hope quickly administered the injection. 'It'll take a moment or two to take effect.'

Mandy felt tears prick her eyes, as she willed the little horse not to give up. 'Try. Please, try.'

'Give me a hand!' Mr Hope said to Wilfred. 'Let's try and get her up. Keep on encouraging her, Mandy.'

'Try and get up,' Mandy urged. 'Come on, Matty. Try for Rose.'

Matty whickered and heaved herself on to her knees.

'She's doing it!' Mandy said. 'Good girl. Almost there!'

Matty swayed. Mandy encouraged. Mr Hope and Wilfred pushed and pulled and finally, shakily, Matty stood up.

'Well done!' exclaimed Mandy, flinging her arms round Matty's neck.

'We're not out of the woods yet,' Mr Hope said. 'I think I'd better prepare to operate—'

'No, wait!' Mandy cried. 'I think the drench is working . . .'

And it was. With a shudder, her legs quivering, Matty began ridding herself of the blockage. Mr Hope, Wilfred, and Mandy stood out of the way while nature took its course. A few minutes later, the elderly mare pricked up her ears and swung round to look at Mandy. She seemed to be saying, 'I did it!'

'Clever girl!' Mandy said. 'Look. The swelling in her tummy's all gone down.'

'By, lass!' Wilfred's wrinkled face was split in a grin. 'I didn't think she'd make it. Thank goodness!'

Mr Hope took one look around Matty's make-shift stall. He put a hand on Mandy's shoulder. 'Thank goodness, indeed . . . for your grandad's straw!'

They all laughed with relief. No one minded the mess or the strong smell. The only thing that mattered was Matty: Matty looking bright-eyed and almost back to her old self.

'Better start clearing up,' Mandy said, feeling as if she could walk on air. 'It'll be just like doing the chores at Animal Ark . . . times ten!'

Mr Hope checked Matty over thoroughly. The little mare seemed remarkably calm after her ordeal. She stood in clean straw. She had drunk some water and was now nibbling at her hay-net.

'Look at her,' Wilfred said fondly. He turned to Mandy. 'Thanks, lass.'

'I didn't do very much,' she replied, blushing.

'No, lass. No need to be modest,' Wilfred said stoutly. 'You gave Matty the will to keep going, just like Rose would have done.'

Mandy was glad she had been able to make a difference. It was a good feeling to think that Rose would have been pleased.

Mr Hope promised to call by the following day, just to make sure Matty hadn't developed any other problems. 'Not that I expect her to,' he said to Wilfred. He waved to the old man as he and Mandy made their way to the Land-rover. 'I'll think about what we said. If I hear of anything, I'll let you know.'

'Right you are!' Wilfred called out.

'What did you mean?' Mandy asked. 'Are you

going to help Wilfred find stabling for Matty?'

Her dad shook his head. 'Back there, in Wilfred's kitchen. He told me how bad he felt about Matty getting sick.'

'But it wasn't Wilfred's fault! Horses can get colic for all sorts of reasons.'

'I know that, love. And Wilfred probably knows it too, but I think he blames himself for being too sentimental, giving in to the impulse to keep Matty for a little while longer.'

Mandy couldn't help herself. She sprang to Wilfred's defence. 'But he loves Matty so much – he just couldn't bear to part with her. And Matty loves Wilfred too, Dad!'

'I know, love,' her dad agreed. 'But now Wilfred thinks he made a bad decision. He knows it's not fair to keep Matty in the house. He has to find her a good home elsewhere. It's the only answer.'

Mandy's spirits sank. 'Wilfred's going to give Matty up, isn't he? And he's asked you to help him find someone to take her!'

Mr Hope nodded. 'It's probably for the best all round.'

Mandy couldn't make herself believe that. What had Wilfred said? 'Us two old 'uns rub along well together.'

She stared out of the window. After everything

that had just happened, poor Wilfred was going to lose his Matty. She felt a tightness in her throat. It wasn't fair. Life wasn't fair. There just had to be some way for Wilfred to keep Matty.

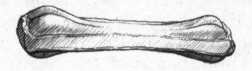

Ten

The following day was a scorchingly hot Sunday. Flora Pearson poured tea into the bright yellow mug and added a generous splash of milk. 'There you are, Sparky.'

Mandy and James grinned as the little dog lapped up his tea. Even on such a hot day, he liked his tea – just like his owner! They had stopped off at the pet shop in Walton, earlier in the week, and bought Sparky a present: a bone-shaped dog chew.

'Oh, how lovely,' Flora said when she saw it. 'Say "thank you" nicely now, Sparky.'

Sparky scooted up on to one haunch. He sat up crookedly and gave one of his startling doggy grins. 'Woof! Woof!'

'Well done,' Flora exclaimed. 'A perfect gentleman!'

They all laughed. 'That special plastic bandage is so clever,' Flora said. 'It supports his leg, but hardly restricts his movements at all.'

'That's why Dad used the vetcast instead of plaster,' Mandy said. 'He says it's a brilliant invention.'

Flora took a sip of her tea. Today she was resplendent in a blue baseball cap and a black T-shirt, which sported an enormous pink pig wearing sunglasses. The logo beneath it read, 'Save my Bacon'.

Mandy and James, both wearing shorts, sprawled on the grass, drinking glasses of cool lemonade. Their bikes were propped against a tree. Sunlight shimmered on the tents and camper vans. The heat haze trembled at the edge of the field.

Flora had rolled up the bottom of her tent and fly-sheet, securing the fabric with plastic clothes pegs, so that cool air blew into the stuffy tent. 'Sparky can't abide being hot when he's resting on his bed,' she explained.

Just then a ball came bouncing towards Flora's tent. Two young children had been kicking it to each other a few yards away. James stood up and kicked the ball back to them. 'Here you are!'

'Thanks!' they called, running to pick it up, their shiny, pink faces wreathed in smiles.

'Hey!' a voice rang out. 'You shouldn't be kicking that around in here. You could damage the tents!' A big man wearing green shorts and a matching shirt stood in front of a posh tent, waving angrily.

The children's faces fell. They scooped up their ball and slunk away down the field.

'Oh, what a shame!' Mandy said. 'They weren't doing any harm.'

'No,' Flora agreed. 'There's little enough for them to do in this field.'

Mandy looked at the children, now sitting on the grass looking bored. She thought how nice it would be if there were some activity provided for them, like a game of volleyball or a paddling pool or maybe riding lessons . . .

'I wonder where Sam Western is,' said James, breaking through Mandy's thoughts. He was looking towards the Range-rover that was parked some way down the field, near the newly-converted shower block. It had been there for some time, but there had been no sign of its driver.

'If you mean the loud-mouth with the waxed jacket and his ferret-faced side-kick,' Flora said with a sniff, 'they're fixing one of the showers. I saw them go in a while ago.'

Mandy and James grinned at each other. Flora's descriptions were colourful, but accurate. Except, Mandy thought, that she was being a bit unfair to ferrets. She was looking idly at the Range-rover, when she caught a movement in the back.

She stiffened and looked at the vehicle more carefully. Yes, all the windows appeared to be shut. And there was the movement again.

'Did Mr Western have his dogs with him?' she asked urgently.

'Yes.' Flora blinked at her. 'Two brutish-looking bulldogs wearing studded collars. Nasty things. They growled at Sparky as the car passed by him.'

Mandy got to her feet. 'Come on!' she yelled.

'What's wrong?' James gaped, scrambling to his feet.

'The windows are all shut,' she called back to him. 'With the sun on it, that Range-rover will be like an oven inside.'

'Oh, heavens!' Flora clapped her hands to her face, catching on quickly. 'Those dogs!'

'Cripes!' James sprinted after Mandy.

Mandy reached the Range-rover first. One look and her worst suspicions were confirmed. Both dogs were collapsed on to their sides, panting and wheezing. Their chests were shuddering painfully, and their tongues trailed limply from the sides of their mouths.

'It's heat exhaustion,' Mandy said. 'I'll get the car keys!' She ran into the old stable block.

Sam Western was talking to two campers, Dennis Saville by his side. 'Quick,' she yelled. 'Mr Western. Come and open your Range-rover!'

'Now just hold on a minute . . .' began Dennis Saville, taking a step towards her.

'Please,' Mandy gasped, ignoring him and grabbing Sam Western's jacket sleeve. 'Your dogs have heatstroke. They could die!'

Sam Western's ruddy face blanched. 'Oh, no!' He rummaged in his pocket and produced the keys, then hurried towards the door.

'Call Animal Ark on your mobile phone,' Mandy said to Dennis Saville. 'It's 703267.' As soon as she saw him dialling the number, she spun on her heel and grabbed a small, plastic wastebin. Dumping the contents on the floor, she filled the bin with water, then charged back outside.

Moments later, Dennis Saville pounded after her. Flora and James were still standing by the Range-rover. Fingers trembling, Sam Western fitted the keys in the lock and dragged open the car door.

A wave of heat hit Mandy in the face.

'The poor things!' James murmured.

The bulldogs didn't look fierce and aggressive now, just distressed: two slumped muscular bodies, their breathing laboured and rasping; faces all made up of tight wrinkles; and huge jaws, hanging open to expose swollen tongues. Mandy felt for them. She might not like their owner, but right now these dogs were just like any other patients needing help.

Suddenly Dennis Saville shouldered her to one side. 'I'll deal with this,' he said curtly. 'Someone give me a hand to lift them out and lay them on the grass.'

'No, wait!' Mandy cried. 'Please!' She jostled for position as Dennis leaned forward. 'Mr Western! First we have to lower their temperature. Right now. Or they could die!'

Saville faltered. He looked across at Sam Western. 'Boss?'

Sam Western shook his head. His neat grey-blond quiff stood on end. For once in his life he seemed lost for words.

'Bulldogs have breathing problems anyway,' Mandy spoke fast, her eyes pleading. 'This is worse for them than other dogs!'

Suddenly a thin figure thrust itself between them. 'Look here!' Flora said, all elbows and indignation. 'I'd advise you two to stop blustering and let Mandy get on with helping those poor dogs! She knows what she's doing. She helped save my Sparky the other night.' Without waiting for their reply, she turned to Mandy. 'What can we do to help, dear?'

Sam Western and Dennis Saville stood aside, their expressions grim.

Mandy sighed in relief. 'We need cloths,' she said. 'Anything we can soak.'

'Here you are!' Flora whipped off her huge T-shirt. She thrust it at Mandy, her skinny arms hanging out of an army surplus vest. James did the same.

Mandy grabbed both T-shirts, dunked them in the water she'd brought out, and laid one across each dog. 'Can you open all the car doors, Mr Western?' she said. 'So that a cool draught blows through.'

'Right.' Sam Western hurried around to the other car doors.

Mandy spoke softly to the stricken dogs. 'Don't worry. Help's coming.' One of them looked at her helplessly, a whimper rising in its throat. Mandy patted its big square head.

Someone gave her a clean handkerchief. Mandy dunked it, then dribbled a little water into the dogs' mouths, not too much or they might choke. Then she dripped water on to the wet T-shirts, keeping them cool.

'I think their breathing's getting a bit easier,' she said after a few moments, wiping their faces with the wet handkerchief. The dogs were panting, their sides heaving like bellows, but the panicked look had gone from their eyes.

Sam Western had taken off his cotton safari jacket and was flapping it about, fanning his dogs. Mandy had never seen him looking so upset. He might be a pompous bully, but he obviously cared deeply for his animals.

'Your dad's here, Mandy!' James cried.

The Animal Ark Land-rover slowed to a halt and Mr Hope jumped out. He took in the situation in a single glance. He nodded to Sam Western then bent over the dogs. After listening to their hearts and lungs he straightened up.

'Will they be all right, Dad?' Mandy asked worriedly.

Her dad smiled. 'I reckon so. You got to them just in time.'

He gave each of the bulldogs a sedative to calm them down. 'If you bring them to the surgery,' he said to Sam Western, 'I'll give them a thorough check-up.'

As he was putting away the syringes, Mr Hope looked up at Sam Western. His normally pleasant face was stern. 'You ought to have known better, Mr

Western,' he said. 'You were minutes away from losing those dogs. Mandy's quick thinking probably saved your dogs' lives.'

Sam Western's face went very red.

'I should say that a thank you was in order,' Flora prompted, digging Mr Western hard in the ribs with a bony elbow.

'Oooof!' he groaned.

Mandy only just managed to suppress a giggle. There was a long pause. Everyone waited. Then Sam Western mumbled, 'Ahem . . . Thank you.'

It was all she was going to get, but Mandy didn't care. The dogs were alive because of her. It was the best feeling in the world. The feeling reminded her why she wanted to be a vet like her mum and dad.

Just then she noticed that the children who had been kicking the ball earlier stood by the car. It had been them who had rushed over and thrust the handkerchief into her hand. An earlier thought came to mind. Yes! There was something important she had to ask Sam Western.

'Mr Western,' she said, making her voice calm and reasonable. 'Can I ask you something?'

Western looked suspicious. 'I suppose so,' he said grudgingly.

Mandy took a deep breath. 'It's about your

campsite. You see – children don't have anything much to do here . . .'

'Hmmph!' Western stuck his hands in his trousers pockets. 'I hadn't planned to make this into a holiday camp, you know! It's only temporary, until I decide what to do with the land.'

Flora gave Western a sharp look. 'I think you should hear Mandy out,' she said, jabbing the air with a thin finger. 'After the huge favour she's just done you!'

Western glanced at Flora nervously. 'Go on then,' he said to Mandy.

'Well – what about offering riding lessons?' Mandy said.

'How would I do that?'

'I think I know someone who might be able to help you out there,' Mandy said. 'I've got a friend who might be able to provide you with the perfect horse . . .'

Sam Western shook his head. 'Sounds like it could be a lot of trouble.'

'It needn't be,' Mandy said, warming to her theme. 'I noticed that there are still two empty stalls in what was the stable block. You could let my friend use one of them for his horse. I'm sure I could persuade him to give free riding lessons to the campers. All you would have to do is provide bedding and food for his horse.'

'It's a good idea,' Mr Hope said, giving his daughter a knowing smile. 'In fact, it's a great idea!'

'That's as may be,' Sam Western said abruptly. 'But I'm still not convinced.'

'I should think you need something to attract people back to the campsite,' Mandy said casually, changing tack.

'What do you mean?' Sam Western asked.

'Well – it can't be good for business – owning a haunted campsite. Free riding lessons would be popular,' Mandy said encouragingly. 'And word would soon get around.'

'You can't argue with that!' Flora said triumphantly.

'No!' agreed James.

Can't he? Mandy thought, *I bet he'll try*! She held her breath. Would Sam Western agree? He was stroking his chin, weighing up the business sense of it. Mandy couldn't bear the suspense.

'OK. I agree.'

'Yes!' James punched the air.

Mandy's own grin spread right across her face. 'That's great! Brilliant! Wait until I tell Wil . . . er, my friend. Oh, there's one more thing . . .'

Sam Western sighed, but his face almost cracked into a smile. Almost. 'Now why am I not surprised? Go on.'

'Well . . .' Mandy began. Sam Western, and

everyone else, listened intently.

When she had finished speaking, Western nodded slowly. 'Mmm . . . Not a bad idea. Not bad at all. I like it!'

Mr Hope lifted Mandy's bike into the back of the Land-rover. 'You know,' he said, giving Mandy one of his lopsided smiles, 'somehow I don't think Sam Western would have been as keen on your idea for riding lessons if he had known that Wilfred was the phantom horseman!'

Mandy chuckled. 'That's why I'm never going to tell him!'

'Me neither!' said James, helping Mandy's dad to slide his bike in beside Mandy's.

'Poor Ernie Bell,' Mandy said thoughtfully, as they drove into Welford. 'He'll have nothing to gossip about, now that the mystery of the ghostly horseman has been solved.'

Her dad grinned. 'Oh, I don't know. I think Ernie will be tickled pink to know that Wilfred's having the last laugh on Sam Western!'

Late afternoon sunshine beamed down on to the old stable block. It was the following day. Mandy and James had rushed over to the campsite after school. There was hardly a cloud in the sky.

'A perfect day for moving in!' Mandy exclaimed.

Wilfred smiled. 'It is that, lass. And it's thanks to you that we are.'

Mandy patted Matty. The little mare was fully recovered; her silver-grey coat gleamed with health. She was reaching down to nibble at the grass, making soft tearing sounds.

'You should thank Sam Western,' she said. 'He saw that the idea made good business sense.'

'Nay.' Wilfred winked. 'I was right first time, lass.'

Mandy remembered his face when she first told him the news yesterday. He had looked at her in disbelief, not sure whether to laugh or cry. 'Eeeh, that's grand,' was all he could say for ages. 'I can keep my Matty? Eeeh, lass. That's grand.'

Mandy had felt a lump rise in her throat. She was happy for Wilfred and happy that she and James could visit Matty whenever they wanted.

'Shall we show Matty her new home?' asked James now.

After having a final check that neither Sam Western nor his men were still about, Wilfred led Matty inside the old stable block. The mare's nostrils quivered and she lifted her head, whickering with pleasure.

'She recognises her old home!' Mandy chuckled. 'Oh, look. Isn't it lovely?'

And it was. A partition had been put in, so that Matty's stall was separate from the toilets and washroom area. There was sweet straw bedding, a full hay-net and fresh water. Sam Western hadn't wasted any time. His workmen must have been busy all day.

'And look!' James said. 'The other empty stall's become a tack room!'

'Oh.' Mandy looked with delight at the straps hanging on hooks, the rack holding saddle soap, cloths, and a stable rubber. Matty's saddle was slung across a sort of bench, topped by a sloping bar. It was perfect. Absolutely perfect.

'Western's outdone himself,' Wilfred said gruffly. 'I'd never have believed it.'

'It's because of his dogs,' said James. 'It's his way of saying thanks.'

Perhaps it was. Mandy felt embarrassed. She changed the subject. 'There's something else, Wilfred. You were too busy with Matty to notice it as we came through the campsite gateway. But come and look now. Both of you.'

Wilfred followed Mandy, Matty at his side. He looked spry and dapper, in corduroy trousers and dark green waistcoat. His white hair was combed back and a mustard scarf was tucked into the neck of his shirt.

Mandy led Wilfred and Matty back to the campsite entrance. James followed, grinning. Together they pointed to the newly-painted sign next to the gateway.

'Da-da!' they shouted.

The sign read, 'Rose of Yorkshire Campsite'.

Wilfred's face glowed. He swallowed hard. 'Eeeh! That's grand. Champion!'

'Sam Western thought my idea to change the campsite's name made sense,' Mandy explained. 'It would stop people thinking about it being haunted.'

'A new name, a new beginning, eh?' Wilfred said, with a wink. 'Western can think what he likes, but we know who this campsite's named after. Don't we, Matty? *Our* Rose!'

The little mare nodded, her ears swivelling. She whickered and blew gently, then butted her nose against Wilfred's smart waistcoat.

'Looks like Matty's given her new home her seal of approval!' Mandy said and she laughed out loud.

PANDA IN THE PARK
Animal Ark in Danger, 38

Lucy Daniels

Mandy Hope's mum is spending some time abroad with a wildlife conservation organisation – and Mandy and James have been offered the chance of a lifetime: to stay with Mrs Hope during the school holidays and help protect endangered animals!

Soon after their arrival in China, Mandy and James spot a lone panda cub near the research park they are visiting. Mrs Hope warns them that the mother panda might reject her baby if they are apart for long. It's vital that the cub and his mother are quickly reunited if he is to be saved. And time is running out . . .

TIGER ON THE TRACK
Animal Ark in Danger, 39

Lucy Daniels

Mandy Hope's mum is spending some time abroad with a wildlife conservation organisation – and Mandy and James have been offered the chance of a lifetime: to stay with Mrs Hope during the school holidays and help protect endangered animals!

Mandy and James are visiting a tiger reserve in India, when the mother of young tigers, Bada and Chhota, goes missing. Other tigers have disappeared too, and poachers are suspected. Mandy and James are determined to help track down the real culprits. But is it too late to save the missing tigers?

GORILLA IN THE GLADE
Animal Ark in Danger, 40

Lucy Daniels

Mandy Hope's mum is spending some time abroad with a wildlife conservation organisation – and Mandy and James have been offered the chance of a lifetime: to stay with Mrs Hope during the school holidays and help protect endangered animals!

While visiting the Kahuzi National Park in Central Africa, Mandy and James help look after Jojo, an adorable baby gorilla who has been abandoned by his mother. Another female gorilla, with a newborn baby of her own, has been picked out as a potential surrogate mum. But will she be willing to take Jojo on?

Join the Animal Action Club!

If you like *Animal Ark*® then you'll love the RSPCA's Animal Action Club! Anyone under 13 can become a member for just £8 a year. Join up and you can look forward to six issues of *Animal Action* magazine – each one is bursting with news, competitions, features, celebrity interviews and a great poster! Plus we'll send you a fab joining pack and a **FREE** RSPCA *Perfect Pets* cuddly toy (worth £4.99) too!!

To join, simply complete the form below – a photocopy is fine – and send it with a cheque for £8 (made payable to RSPCA) to RSPCA Animal Action Club, Wilberforce Way, Southwater, Horsham, West Sussex RH13 9RS. We'll then send your joining pack, free toy and first issue of *Animal Action*.

Don't delay, join today!

Name:

Address:

Postcode:	Date of birth:

Signature of parent/guardian: